Zur Einführung

Ob „Anfänger" oder „Fortgeschrittener", jeder macht Fehler, die manchmal zu Verständnisschwierigkeiten beim englischsprachigen Gesprächspartner führen können. Jeder möchte perfekt sprechen – es liegen aber manche Stolpersteine im Weg: oft fehlt die richtige Aussprache, das passende Wort, die treffende Formulierung. Auch die eigene Muttersprache bereitet Probleme beim Englischlernen – man kann nicht alles wortwörtlich ins Englische übertragen, und manche deutschen Wörter sehen aus wie englische, haben aber häufig eine ganz andere Bedeutung. Also Vorsicht bei diesen „falschen Freunden"!

Mit **Teste dein Englisch 1** können Sie Ihre Englischkenntnisse systematisch ausbauen. Die 14 Kapitel steigern sich vom Einfachen zum Schwierigen und testen etwa den Stoff, der dem ersten Jahr des Volkshochschullehrplans entspricht. Es ist aber durchaus auch möglich, die Kapitel in beliebiger Reihenfolge durchzuarbeiten, falls Sie andere Schwerpunkte setzen wollen.

Teste dein Englisch 1 enthält eine Vielfalt von verschiedenen Übungen für die wichtigsten Problemfälle deutschsprachiger Englischlerner: Das Verb und seine Zeitformen, Präpositionen, Aussprache und Intonation, Fragestellung, Wortschatz, Landeskunde und Leseverstehen.
Die einzelnen Kapitel, die Units, sind so gestaltet, dass sie ein zwangloses Lernen ermöglichen, auch unterwegs oder wenn nur wenig Zeit zur Verfügung steht, z. B. in der Mittagspause. Jede Unit kann in 15–20 Minuten durchgearbeitet werden.

Wir wünschen Ihnen viel Spaß und viel Erfolg!

Inhaltsverzeichnis

Meeting People

UNIT 1

1 Greetings

Which go together?

1 How do you do?
2 How are you?
3 Hello, I'm Chris.
4 What's your name?
5 Are you from Germany?
6 Hi!

a Yes, I am.
b Hello, pleased to meet you. I'm Heinz.
c How do you do?
d Tony.
e Hi!
f Fine thanks. And you?

2 My family

Put in the right words.

My name . . . . Christopher. I . . . . from Germany. I . . . . English, from London. Look, here . . . . a photo of my family. This . . . . my wife, Ulrike. She . . . . . from England. She . . . . German. These . . . . our children. They . . . . at school yet. They . . . . too young. And that . . . . our dog, Toby.

's isn't 'm 'm not 's is 's are aren't 's are

3 Where or Who?

Put in the right word.

1 . . . . . are you from?

2 . . . . . is that woman over there?

3 . . . . . do you live?

4 . . . . . is my pen?

5 . . . . . can help me?

6 . . . . . do you work?

4 Nationalities

Here are the nationalities – what are the countries?

1 Italian ....

2 Scottish ....

3 English ....

4 German ....

5 French ....

6 Greek ....

7 Turkish ....

8 Spanish ....

9 American ....

10 Portuguese ....

5 A star

I'm Tony. And, yes, I've got a nickname: Tonedeaf! I'm from London, and I've got a small house with a garden. I've got a dog. His name's Sinatra because he's got a good voice! I've got one brother and two sisters. Their names are James: he's fifteen, Sarah: she's thirteen, and Tracy: she's eight. My hobbies? Well, music is my hobby. I've got about two hundred CDs. My room? I've got a lot of posters and my stereo, hundreds of cassettes, records and music videos. Teddy bears? Yes, I've got Mr. B! He's my number one bear!

Answer the questions with short answers.

1 Is Tony from London? ....
2 Has he got a nickname? ....
3 Has he got a flat? ....
4 Is Sarah thirteen? ....
5 Is Tracy nine? ....
6 Is football his hobby? ....
7 Has he got a lot of CDs? ....
8 Has he got a TV in his room? ....

6 Numbers 1

What are the numbers? Write them down.

1 seven ....
2 twenty-one ....
3 thirteen ....
4 thirty ....
5 forty-three ....
6 twelve ....
7 eighty-four ....
8 ninety-six ....
9 seventy-eight ....
10 fifty-nine ....

7 Numbers 2

What are the numbers? Write them down.

1 14 ....

2 40 ....

3 56 ....

4 93 ....

5 37 ....

6 73 ....

7 85 ....

8 58 ....

9 62 ....

10 26 ....

8 Sounds 1

Which words sound the same? (Only four pairs are possible.)

there	**here**	**this**	**these**	**those**	**buy**	**their**	**bye**		
meet	**kiss**	**be**	**his**	**her**	**met**	**the**	**hear**	**meat**	

1 ....

2 ....

3 ....

4 ....

9 Sounds 2

Which words have the same sound in the middle?

hat	**head**
. . . .	. . . .
. . . .	. . . .
. . . .	. . . .
. . . .	. . . .
. . . .	. . . .
. . . .	. . . .
. . . .	. . . .

cat bed fat wet sat pet had said that Pat flat set fed

10 Prepositions

Put in the right words.

at to from for in in at

1 I come . . . . Germany.

2 I live . . . . London.

3 I work . . . . an American firm.

4 Look . . . . this photo.

5 I live . . . . a big house.

6 My husband is . . . . home all day.

7 Can I introduce you . . . . my husband, David?

11 Pairs

Which words go together?

this	England	isn't	eight	cat	hello	goodbye
English	that	is	dog	eighty		

1 ....

2 ....

3 ....

4 ....

5 ....

6 ....

12 Polite and impolite

Which is more polite?

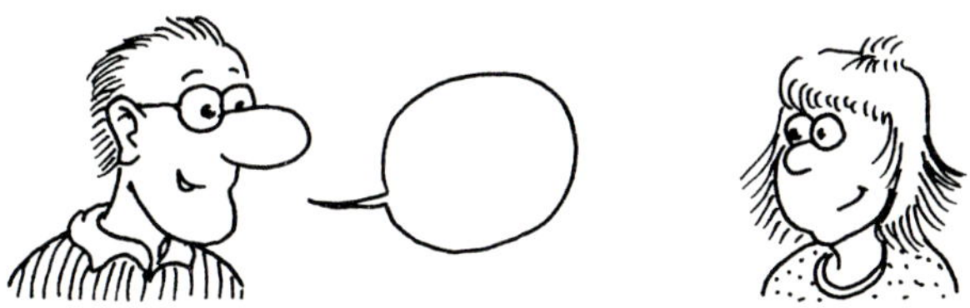

1 Who are you? ▢
Hello, I'm Bernd. What's your name? ▢

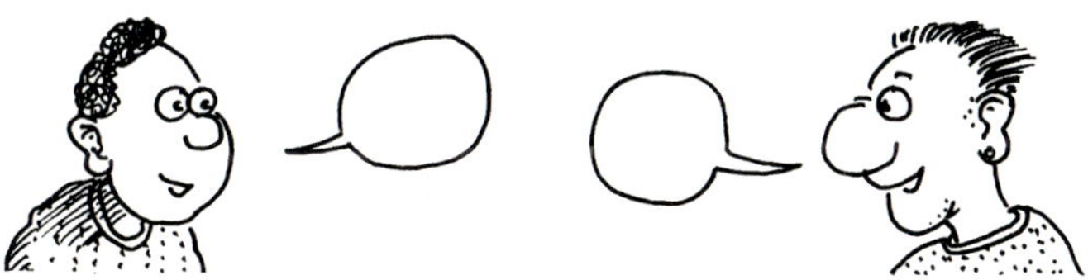

2 Are you from Germany? ▢
Yes. ▢
Yes, I am. ▢

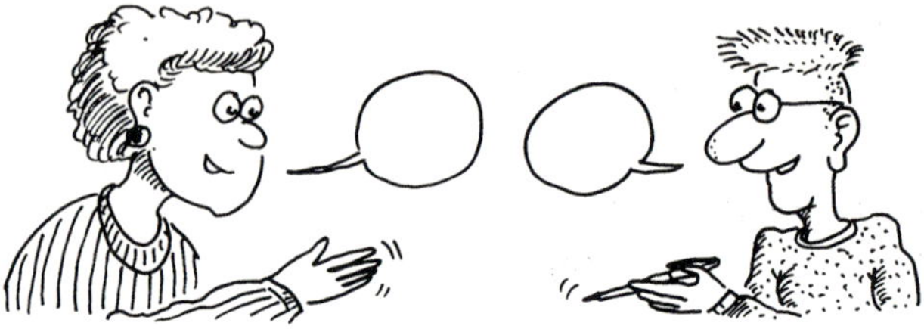

3 Can I have your pen? ▢
Give me your pen. ▢
4 Here you are. ▢
Here. ▢

13 *a* or *an*?

Put in the right one.

1 . . . . friend
2 . . . . English friend
3 . . . . American book
4 . . . . German book
5 . . . . empty room
6 . . . . bathroom
7 . . . . unit

Home Sweet Home

UNIT 2

1 Two women

Make a dialogue from the jumbled words. (The sentences are in the right order.)

got children you any have?

. . . .

have yes, I .

. . . .

got children how have many you ?

. . . .

daughter got and sons I've one two .

. . . .

nice oh, that's .

. . . .

you what about ? you family got a have ?

. . . .

I've boyfriend got but a any we children got haven't .

. . . .

you lucky! busy always so I'm the with kids. time just I got for much myself haven't .

. . . .

. . . .

plenty got of I've time! job my got boyfried a has good free he got time a lot of has .

. . . .

. . . .

always husband work is my at! never any got time the for he's family !

. . . .

. . . .

2 A letter

*Put in the right forms of **have/has got**.*

Dear David, July 14th

Thanks for your last letter. I .... some really good news! I .... a new girlfriend! Her name's Sarah. She's wonderful! You must meet her. She .... big, blue eyes and a beautiful smile! I .... (not) much time for other things at the moment, we're always together.

.... (you) time next week? Perhaps we can meet. She .... an evening off next Wednesday (She .... a job as a nurse and .... (not) a lot of time in the evenings). How is Jill? .... (still) that bad cold, or is she better now? Send her my regards. And what about you? .... any plans for your Summer holidays? Sarah and I .... lots of plans! I'll tell you more later. Ring me or write me a note if you .... a moment.

All the best,
Adrian

3 Gary, the megastar

Answer the questions (use short answers).

1 Has Gary got a lot of money? (+)

. . . .

2 Has he got a fast car? (+)

. . . .

3 Has Gary got any friends? (–)

. . . .

4 Has he got a luxury home? (+)

. . . .

5 Has he got any children? (–)

. . . .

6 Has he got a lot of fans? (+)

. . . .

7 Have his fans got all his records? (+)

. . . .

8 Have his fans got his address? (–)

. . . .

9 Has he got much time? (–)

. . . .

10 Has he got any hair? (–)

. . . .

4 An interview with Gary.

Look at the reporter's notes. What are the reporter's questions?

1 "Have you got a big house?"

2 "How many rooms has . . . . ?"

3 " . . . . ?"

4 " . . . . ?"

5 " . . . . ?"

6 " . . . . ?"

7 " . . . . ?"

8 " . . . . ?"

5 House ads

Read the advertisements. Which picture goes with which advertisement?

1 **Beautiful detached house** with large back garden. **Three bedrooms**, kitchen, bathroom with separate WC. **Large living room** with view of garden. Gas central heating.

2 Small but **cosy terraced house**. Ten minutes from city centre. **Two bedrooms**, living room, kitchen, bath with WC. Small back yard.

3 **Semidetached house** for sale. **Two bedrooms**, living room, dining room, kitchen, bath with WC. **Small front garden** and larger back garden with garden shed. Bus stop to city at end of street.

A

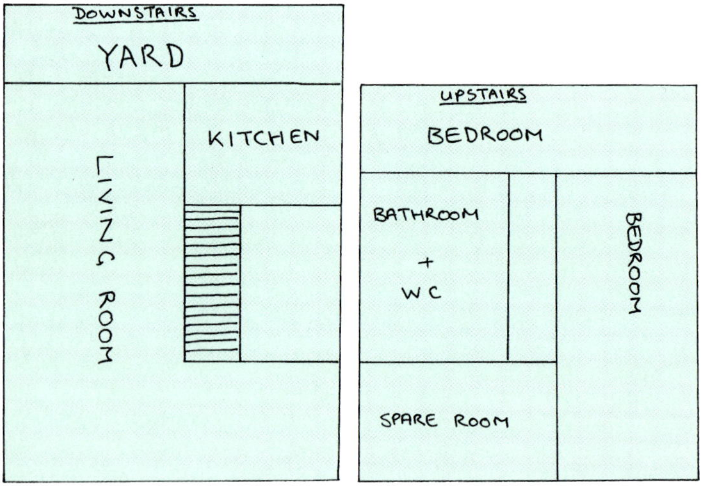

B

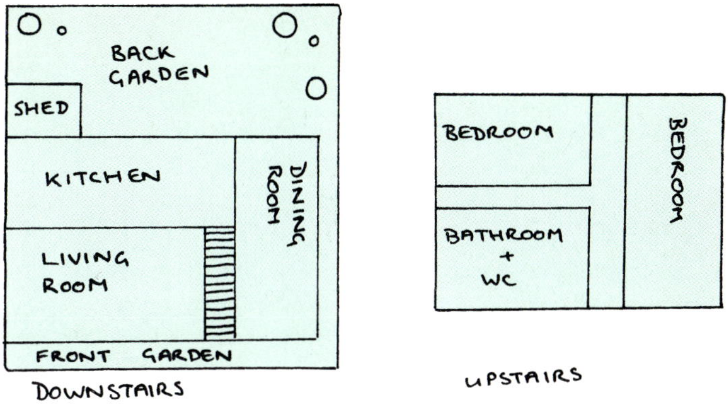

C

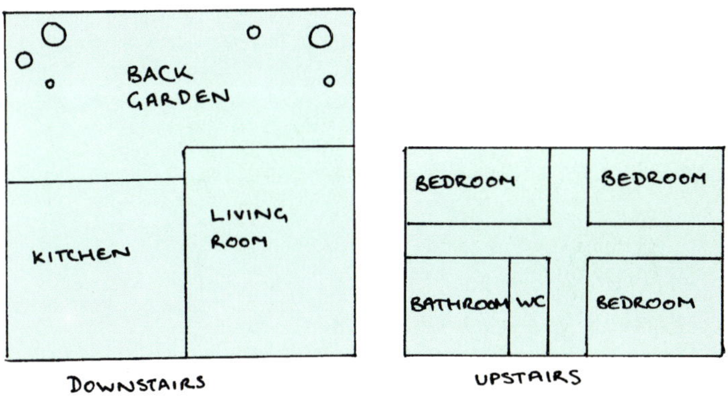

1 is picture . . . . . 2 is picture . . . . . 3 is picture . . . . .

Which of these statements are right or wrong?	**R**	**W**
1 The first house has got a dining room.		
2 The first house hasn't got a front garden.		
3 The second house has got a small garden.		
4 The second house isn't far from the city centre.		
5 The third house is in the city centre.		
6 The third house has got a large front garden.		

6 A family

Put in the right pronouns.

Gavin Richards lives in Norwich. . . . . . . has got a small house ten minutes from the centre. It has got a beautiful garden with flowers and trees. ". . . . . . . work in . . . . at weekends, when . . . . have got time. . . . .'s my hobby." Gavin is separated from his wife. ". . . . . . . lives near here. Her house is just round the corner. . . . . meet quite a lot, and . . . . go out together. . . . . phone just about every day. . . . . . . 's a friendly relationship." Gavin's wife lives with their son, Ben, aged ten. Gavin sees . . . . a lot, too. "Ben helps . . . . with the gardening. . . . .'s very good at . . . .! Ben has got both of . . . ., his father *and* his mother."
Ben says: ". . . . . . . like . . . . . . .both. . . . . are my mum and dad. But we don't live in one house. That's a pity."

I (x 4) **me** **she** **her** **he** (x 2) **him** **it** (x 4)
we (x 2) **us** **they** **them**

7 Scenes at home

What are the right words? Put them in.

1 We live quite . . . . the city centre.
(by – at – near – in the near of – in)

2 Our house is . . . . Green Street.
(on – at – along – in)

3 That's our house. We live . . . . number 37.
(at – into – to)

4 Come on. Let's go . . . . the living room
(at – into – for – out)

5 Lisa, my wife, is . . . . the kitchen, I think.
(into – at – by – in)

6 She's always . . . . home when I'm . . . . work.
(at – to – by/at – to – by)

7 Please, sit . . . .
(in – into – down)

8 That's Tina, our cat, She's always . . . . the sofa or

. . . . the fire!
(on – at – down/in – in front of – on)

9 Look . . . . the window.
(in – out of – for – to)

10 That's my daughter there . . . . the garden.
(at – in – into – by)

11 You see that picture . . . . the wall?
(at – onto – over – on)

12 That's my other daughter, Melissa. She's . . . .
Germany at the moment.
(at – in – over)

13 Look . . . . this old photo. It's our old house.
(on – at – in – onto)

14 That's my father . . . . the picture. He's dead now.
(on – at – from – in)

15 My mother lives . . . . the park.
(at – in the near – by – into)

8 This, that, these, those

Put in the right words.

Bruce: Let me show you around the house. Walk . . . . way. Now, ... is our living room here. . . . . is our dog, Scamp, over there on the sofa. Get off, Scamp!

Steve: Is . . . . your son in . . . . photo on the wall over there?

Bruce: Yes, it is. Trevor. He's in America . . . . year.

Steve: . . . .'s nice.

Bruce: Look at . . . . photo here. . . . . are my parents. They live next door.

Steve: What? In . . . . big house! Lovely. Isn't it too big for the two of them?

Bruce: Another couple live downstairs. Look out of the window. You see . . . . two windows at the top of the house over there? . . . . is where my father does his painting.

Steve: Oh, he's an artist!

Bruce: Yes, he's quite good. . . . . painting here is by him, but. . . . . two little pictures over there are my favourite ones.

Steve: I paint a bit, too. You know . . . . picture in my office? . . . .'s one of mine.

9 Home

What are the words?

10 Words

Which adjectives can't describe the words? Cross them out.

People: friendly, interesting, happy, expensive, helpful, empty
Garden: beautiful, kind, young, handsome, small, boring
House: pretty, young, expensive, helpful, big, kind
Sofa: comfortable, sad, beautiful, expensive, helpful

11 A guest

Which go together?

1 Can I introduce you to my wife, Helen. ▢
2 This is Peter, my son. ▢
3 Lovely home you've got! ▢
4 You must be John's daughter. ▢
5 How are you? ▢

a Hello, your father has told me a lot about you.
b That's right.
c Oh, thank you very much!
d Fine thanks, and you?
e Pleased to meet you, Mrs Taylor.

12 Sounds

Put the words under the right heading.

bread aunt fast bed bath end class head half lesson car men answer

ɑː	e
father	**friend**
....	....
....	....
....	....
....	....
....	....
....	....

13 German words, English words

Here are some German words. What are they in English?

1 Adresse ....

2 Musik ....

3 Nummer ....

4 Papier ....

5 Telefon ....

6 neu ....

7 Onkel ....

8 Garten ....

9 Idee ....

10 Familie ....

14 Crossword: The family

Clues: Down

1 Joan is Jim's . . . .

2 Hilda is Joan's . . . .

3 Hilda is Simon's . . . .

4 What Simon calls Joan . . .

5 Bernie is Simon's . . . .

6 John is Diana's . . . .

7 Simon is Jim's . . . .

8 Jim is Bernie's . . . .

Clues: Across

9 Ted is Joan's . . . .

10 Sarah is Joan's . . . .

11 Joan is Ted and Hilda's . . .

12 Diana is Sarah's . . . .

13 Bernie is Joan's . . . .

14 What Simon calls Ted . . .

UNIT 3 In Town, Out of Town

1 A tourist 1

Answer the stranger's questions with short answers.

1 "Is there a tourist information office near here?"

. . . .

2 "Are there any pubs around here?"

. . . .

3 "Is there a police station near here?"

. . . .

4 "Are there any museums in the town?"

. . . .

5 "Is there a supermarket near here?"

. . . .

6 "I'm looking for a newsagent's. Are there any around here?"

. . . .

2 A tourist 2

Now you are the tourist. Ask the questions.

1 . . . .
Yes, there is. There's a book shop in King Street.

2 . . . .
No, there isn't. We haven't got a florist's in town.

3 . . . .
No, there aren't any art galleries here at all.

4 . . . .
A baker's? I think there's one in Queen's Road.

5 . . . .
Yes, there are. There's Brown's restaurant in Queen's Road and another one in Park Road.

6 . . . .
An underground station? Not round here!

3 A new home

Put in ***some*** *or* ***any****.*

Dear Jenny,

We're in our new house now; it's super! We haven't got .... curtains yet, but we've got .... really wonderful furniture: a sofa, two arm-chairs, a dining table and .... chairs. The street's quite quiet. There isn't .... traffic at night, but there are .... noisy neighbours next door! They're quite friendly, but they often have friends round, and they play .... very loud music at times. There is a nice Pakistani family across the street, though. They've got .... sweet children! I don't think they've got .... friends around here. They're happy to meet .... new people, like us. What about you? Have you got .... news?

4 An evening out

Put in the verb in the right form.

AN EVENING OUT?

"My husband? He just .... (stay) at home in the evening and .... (watch) TV! We never do anything!"

"Well, my wife .... (like) the theatre, so we go into the city a lot."

"My wife always .... (listen) to the radio. It's terrible! She never .... (want) to go to a concert or to a disco."

"Nothing! He .... (do) nothing! I do all the work and he just .... (sit) there! We haven't got a social life."

"My husband is wonderful! He .... (hurry) back from work and then .... (help) me with the housework. He never .... (relax)! But he never .... (have) any time to go out with me!"

"I love my missus. She never .... (try) to tell me what to do! So I go out every evening."

"When my husband .... (come) back from the pub, he always .... (kiss) me and .... (say): Sorry I'm late, dear!"

5 Thomas and Adrian

Write about the two men.

Thomas	**Adrian**
lives in a town	lives in a village
plays tennis	listens to classical music
likes dancing	plays chess
goes out a lot	stays at home a lot
reads magazines	reads books
watches TV	collects stamps

1 *Adrian doesn't live in a town.*

2 *Thomas doesn't live in a village.*

3 ....

4 ....

5 ....

6 ....

7 ....

8 ....

9 ....

10 ....

11 ....

12 ....

6 Staying in and going out

What are the questions?

QUESTIONNAIRE

1 . . . . (sports)?
Yes, I do. I do a lot of sports.

2 . . . .
. . . . (What sports)?
I play tennis and go jogging

3 . . . .
. . . . (go out with friends)?
Yes, I do. I go out with my friends a lot.

4 . . . .
. . . . (ever – go to the theatre)?
No, I don't. I never go to the theatre.

5 . . . .
. . . . (watch films at the cinema)?
No, I don't. I don't like cinemas.

6 . . . .
. . . . (go to restaurants)?
Yes, I do. I really like going to restaurants.

7 . . . .
. . . . (go for walks)?
Yes, I do. I often go out for walks in the park.

8 . . . .
. . . . (drive to work)?
No, I don't. I haven't got a car. I go by bus.

9 . . . .
. . . . (watch TV)?
Yes, I do. I always watch the football on TV.

7 A place to live

stately home – a large country house, usually of historical interest and containing fine works of art, especially one which people pay to visit.
semidetached house – one of a pair of joined houses
detached house – one not connected on any side with any other building
terraced house – house which is part of a row of houses, or terrace
bedsitter – a small, one-room flat
bungalow – a fairly modern house built only on one level
cottage – a small, old house especially in the country
block of flats – a large building separated into a number of flats

Where do they live? Match the statements to the descriptions.

1 "I never go out much. I'm too frightened. There are lots of young people on the stairs and the lift is always out of order. Too many bad people live here".

. . . .

2 "It's wonderful here. The good air, the peace and quiet, no traffic. Our house isn't very big, but it's beautiful!"

. . . .

3 "The only problem is with our neighbours. They're so noisy! We can hear them through the wall. Thank God we have no neighbours on the other side of the house!"

. . . .

4 "Well of course, I love this place. My family has always lived here. In summer thousands of tourists come here, but, well, we need the money!"

. . . .

5 "I love living here. So many different people live around here. We've got a Pakistani family next door, and a Chinese family on the other side. It's just so interesting!"

. . . .

6 "It's a nice place for the kids. There's a garden all around the house, you see. And it's quite quiet, although we're near the city centre."

. . . .

7 "It's nice here, although we can't go upstairs!"

. . . .

8 "This place is just right for me. I haven't got much money, and I'm out most of the time. I just sleep here, really."

. . . .

LIFE IN THE CITY

LIFE IN THE COUNTRY

8 Going out and staying in

Put the words under the right headings.

Going out	Staying in
....	....
....	....
....	....
....	....
....	....
....	....
....	....
....	....
....	....
....	....

restaurant sofa park jogging chess radio TV cinema walk disco living room relax video tennis club pub lazy

9 Going into town

Put in the right words.

Mrs Burns lives .... the country. (into – in)

She sometimes gets the bus .... town. (into – along)

She goes .... the shops there. (for – to)

When she's .... town, she spends a lot of time .... the supermarket. (into – in/at – through)

She often has a cup of coffee at the cafe .... the supermarket. (next – next to)

Every month she goes to the hairdresser's . . . . King Street. (on – in)

There's a bus stop . . . . the bank (before – in front of), so she walks . . . . the park to get there (between – through)

The bus stop is just . . . . the road from her cottage. (outside – down)

10 *in*

*You can't always translate the German word "**in**" by the English "**in**". Put the right translation into the sentences.*

1 Er geht jeden Tag in die Stadt.
2 Sie wohnt im zweiten Stock.
3 Du kannst es im Supermarkt kaufen.
4 Sie sind im Kino.
5 Willkommen in London!
6 Sie ist im Bus nach Norwich.

1 He goes . . . . town every day.

2 She lives . . . . the second floor.

3 You can buy it . . . . the supermarket.

4 They are . . . . the cinema.

5 Welcome . . . . London!

6 She is . . . . the bus to Norwich.

to **at** (x 2) **into** **on** (x 2)

11 Words together

Which of the words and phrases can go with the words in the list?

go ....

....

do ....

....

watch ....

....

listen to ....

....

a video the shopping to the shops sports CDs out with friends the radio the washing up music the housework for a walk TV by bus a film

12 Sounds: *z* and *s*

Which „S-sound" is different from the other three words?

1	lives	goes	helps	does
2	puts	stays	gets	sits
3	asks	buys	flies	lies
4	brings	sees	sings	makes
5	hates	likes	plays	walks

13 A child's letter

Can you correct the spelling?

1. Dear Granny,

Its nice hear on hollyday. Its a luvly houz. Their are lots of nice things here and a sinema next door and a park down the rode. Mum + Dad are all rite. There in the gardin now with frendz. Today I wont to by a comic. How are you?

Love from Zue

. . . .

. . . .

. . . .

. . . .

14 Puzzle

What are the words?

In town:

s ■ ■ ps ....

b ■ ■ k ....

■ o ■ t o ■ ■ i ■ e ....

■ ■ p ■ rm ■ ■ ■ et ....

■ i ■ e ■ a ....

■ ■ sc ■ ....

r ■ ■ t ■ ■ r ■ ■ t ....

■ u ■ s ■ ■ p ....

■ ar ■ ....

s ■ ■ e ■ t ....

From Day to Day

UNIT 4

1 How do they get to work?

What are they saying?

1 I go . . . .

2 I get to work . . . .

3 I go to work . . . .

4 I always go . . . .

5 Me? I get to work . . . .

2 Way to work

Read the article quickly and answer the questions.

Way to work

Mr James, like thousands of other people who live in London, gets to work by underground. "It's the best way for me to get to my office", he told us. "A lot of people go to work by car, but the traffic in London is terrible in the mornings."

But it's a long journey. He leaves his house at seven fifteen and then walks to the station, near his house. His tube* gets to Covent Garden station at twenty past eight. Then he goes on foot to his office, about ten minutes from the station. "I get to the office just on time", he says, "but sometimes the tube is late. But that's not really important ...", he smiles, ... because I'm the boss!"

* tube = London underground

Right or wrong?

1 A lot of people go to work by underground.	**Right**	**Wrong**
2 Mr James gets to work by car.	**Right**	**Wrong**
3 A lot of people drive to work.	**Right**	**Wrong**
4 Mr James gets up at seven fifteen.	**Right**	**Wrong**
5 His tube arrives at Covent Garden at 8.25.	**Right**	**Wrong**
6 He gets to work at about 8.45.	**Right**	**Wrong**
7 He has got an important job.	**Right**	**Wrong**

3 -s or -'s?

Put in the right one.

1 My wife work . . . . . . in an office.

2 She . . . . . . a secretary.

3 She . . . . . . got a nice boss, and her colleagues are all right, too.

4 I do the shopping because she get . . . . . . home quite late.

5 At the weekend she . . . . . . got time for the family.

6 During the week she . . . . . . always tired in the evening.

7 On Saturday . . . . . . we go out together.

8 That . . . . . . the best day of the week, I think.

9 Our two little boy . . . . . . are often sad because she . . . . . . away all day.

10 I do all the job . . . . . . in the house because I'm out of work.

4 A 7-day week

Look at the housewife's answers and write down the reporter's questions.

1 . . . .
. . . .?

I'm a housewife.

2 . . . .
. . . .?

Yes, it is a hard job. I work every day, and I haven't got any holidays!

3 . . . . ?
I get up at about six o'clock, when my son wakes up.

4 . . . . ?
I make breakfast for the family at about seven o'clock.

5 . . . . ?
I start my housework after breakfast, at about eight o'clock.

6 . . . . ?
Yes, I have one break. For coffee.

7 . . . . ?
My coffee break? At about half past ten.

8 . . . . ?
I cook lunch at half past twelve. My son comes home for lunch, you see.

9 . . . . ?
My husband? He gets home at six thirty.

10 . . . . ?
My son? Well, he gets back from school at about quarter past four.

11 . . . . ?
I watch TV in the evenings. I'm always so tired!

12 . . . . ?
I go to bed at about eleven o'clock.

5 What's the time?

a) Draw the times on the clocks.

1 Half past two
2 Ten to eleven (pm)
3 Quarter past eight
4 Twenty-five to four

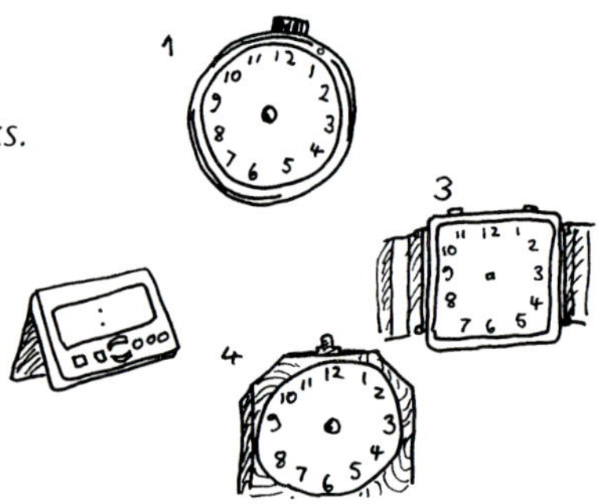

b) Write down the times.

5 ....

6 ....

7 ....

8 ....

6 Prepositions

Put in the right word.

1 I go .... work .... seven o'clock every day.

2 I get back .... work quite late.

3 I have lunch .... 12 and 1.

4 Our tea break is .... 10 .... 10.15.

5 The boss is ...... his office.

6 My husband works .... six o'clock.

7 There are a lot of nice colleagues .... work.

at between until to in from at from ... to

7 The office

Put in the right words.

calculator photocopier desk telephone printer typewriter fax chair computer

8 What's the right translation for *bei*?

1 Er arbeitet **bei** Langenscheidt.

He works . . . . Langenscheidt.

2 Sie ist **bei** der Arbeit.

She is . . . . work.

3 Meine Fabrik liegt **bei** München.

My factory is . . . . Munich.

4 Wenn ich in die Arbeit gehe, sind meine Kinder **bei** meinen Eltern.

When I go to work my children are . . . . my parents'.

5 Ich habe meine Dokumente nicht **bei** mir.

I haven't got my documents . . . . me.

at near with at for

9 Which are the odd words out?

1 nurse doctor waiter engineer typewriter manager teacher

. . . .

2 bus car taxi bike train plane boat tram

. . . .

3 day night afternoon evening week morning

. . . .

4 telephone computer secretary desk chair type-writer fax

. . . .

5 hard boring difficult dangerous interesting dirty

. . . .

10 Which one is the right way to ask what someone's job is?

1 How do you do? ☐
2 What are you doing? ☐
3 What is your work? ☐
4 How are you? ☐
5 What do you do? ☐
6 How's work? ☐

11 *"th"*: Which words have the same sounds?

Put them in the right lists.

that through thirteen rather those father
bath thirty thanks these there throw

ð this	θ three
....	....
....	....
....	....
....	....
....	....
....	....

12 What are the jobs?

1

2

3

4

5

6

7

8

9

UNIT 5 Time for Fun

1 At the sports centre

Put in the right words.

my – mine your – yours his – his her – hers
our – ours their – theirs

1 Is this racket **yours**? No, it isn't . . . . I think it's . . . .
Hey! What are you doing with . . . . racket!?

2 Careful: Their team is very good, especially . . . . striker.

Captain: Yes, but . . . . shirts are nicer than . . . .!

3 Is this . . . . ball? Yes, I think it's . . . .

4 . . . . forehand is better than . . . .

Yes, but he always keeps . . . . eye on the ball!

2 Likes and dislikes.

Put in the right phrases.

1 "I . . . . English food!"

2 "I . . . . playing chess."

3 "I . . . . jogging."

4 "I . . . . German food!"

love   don't like   like   can't stand

3 Lonely Hearts

Find a match! Which people from the two groups have got the same interests?

1 **Man,** 38, tall, dark and handsome. Very active. Likes jogging, skiing and discos.

2 **Young-looking 40 year old male** seeks attractive woman of same age. Must be smoker. Likes going to the cinema. Hates staying at home in front of the TV.

3 **30 year old male** is looking for the woman of his life! Loves volleyball, squash and other indoor games!

4 **Quiet man,** 35, seeks woman (under 30) for pleasant evenings at home. Likes chess, reading and classical music.

a **Home-loving 28 year old woman** seeks man for peaceful hours. Likes Mozart and Victorian literature.

b **Woman, 35** is looking for Mr Right! Likes outdoor sports and dancing.

c **Good-looking princess, 25,** seeks her prince. Loves team sports but smokes, too! Likes quiet evenings in front of the TV!

d **39 year old smoker, female, pretty,** wants to find her dream man. Likes films, hates TV!

1 . . . . 2 . . . . 3 . . . . 4 . . . .

4 Lonely Hearts' Agency

What are the interviewer's questions?

1 . . . . ?
I'm 29 years old.

2 . . . . ?
Yes, I am. I'm a very active person.

3 . . . . ?
Yes, I do. I love sports!

4 . . . . ?
What sports do I do? Well, I play football, and I do body-building.

5 . . . . ?
Any other interests? Yes, I have. I like music.

6 . . . . ?
Yes, I can play an instrument. The piano.

7 . . . . ?
No, I don't. I can't stand classical music!

8 . . . . ?
What sort of music? I like jazz and blues.

9 . . . . ?
I live in Leeds. In a detached house.

10 . . . . ?
What sort of woman do I like? Well, young and beautiful, like you!

11 . . . . ?
Yes, I love going to the cinema.
So do I! How about this evening?

5 Going out

Put in the right question word/s + right form of **do** *in the questions.*

how often who how why when what time where what how much

1 . . . . you go every evening?
To the tennis club.

2 . . . . you play with?
I always play with my boyfriend.

3 . . . . your husband watch TV?
Every day. It's terrible!

4 . . . . the Cezanne exhibition cost?
About £5, I think.

5 . . . . they go on holiday?
They go by train. They haven't got a car.

6 . . . . she like disco music so much? I think it's awful!
Because she loves dancing.

7 . . . . you take your dog for a walk?
Twice a day.

8 . . . . he like about Susan?
Well, she's an active person, like he is. And she's very intelligent.

9 . . . . the film start?
At eight o'clock.

6 Ordinal numbers 1

What are they? Write them down.

1	twenty-first	21st	6	ninety-ninth	. . . .
2	third	. . . .	7	eleventh	. . . .
3	forty-second	. . . .	8	thirteenth	. . . .
4	thirtieth	. . . .	9	thirty-first	. . . .
5	fourth	. . . .	10	sixtieth	. . . .

7 Ordinal numbers 2

What are they? Write them down in words.

1 5th . . . .

2 33rd . . . .

3 12th . . . .

4 40th . . . .

5 14th . . . .

6 51th . . . .

7 22nd . . . .

8 8th . . . .

9 15th . . . .

10 100th . . . .

8 Special dates

There are a number of important dates in the English year which are different from those in Germany, or indeed, do not even exist there. For example, at Christmas, the most important day is Christmas Day. This is on December 25th. It's also the day on which people can open their presents! People usually have their Christmas dinner on this day – not in the evening. December 24th is Christmas Eve in England. Another special date in England is November 5th. On this day – Guy Fawkes Night – people celebrate the day in 1605 when Guy Fawkes tried to blow up Parliament – without success. There are fireworks and usually a large bonfire, on which a "Guy", a figure made of old clothes, is burned. Shrove Tuesday, or "Pancake Day" is the last day before Lent – the forty days before Easter, on which, traditionally, people eat pancakes. Another important day in the year is . . .

What days are in the pictures?

1 . . . .   3 . . . .

2 . . . .   4 . . . .

9 Describing people or things

Which of the words are positive and which are negative?

boring interesting awful bad good terrible friendly unfriendly beautiful dangerous excellent silly fantastic wonderful stupid exciting

+	–
. . . .	. . . .
. . . .	. . . .
. . . .	. . . .
. . . .	. . . .
. . . .	. . . .
. . . .	. . . .

10 Sounds

dʒ **jump** and tʃ **chair**

Which word sounds different?

1	Germany	July	chief	age	. . . .
2	choose	match	January	child	. . . .
3	German	catch	June	general	. . . .
4	question	much	watch	orange	. . . .

11 Making words

Make words with **-er** *and put them in the sentences.*

1 He's a brillant footballer! (football)

2 That's our star tennis . . . . (play) over there.

3 My brother's a very safe . . . . (drive).

4 There are so many . . . . (jog) in the park these days.

5 There are eight . . . . (run) in this race.

6 I like playing with my . . . . (compute).

7 Frank Sinatra is a wonderful . . . . (sing).

8 Look at this picture. My father is a . . . . (paint), you know.

12 Activities

Put the words under the right heading. Some can be in both.

playing tennis   watching TV   playing chess   doing the washing up   playing squash   collecting stamps   jogging   climbing   skiing   basketball   listening to the radio   playing computer games   reading books   sunbathing   bodybuilding

INDOORS	OUTDOORS
....	....
....	....
....	....
....	....
....	....
....	....
....	....
....	....
....	....

13 The right way to say it

Cross out the wrong words.

1 Can you **say** – **tell** me the time, please?
2 Your wife is a very **interested** – **interesting** person.
3 I don't understand. What do you **mean** – **think**?
4 I **mean** – **think** that is a great idea!
5 I'm very **interesting** – **interested** in stamp collecting.
6 In my spare time I **make** – **do** a lot of sport.
7 My friend **tells** – **says** me that you play squash. Is that right?
8 I like **making** – **doing** model planes in my free time.
9 Oh no! I always **do** – **make** the same mistake!
10 My free time? I always **make** – **do** the housework!

14 Puzzle: Activities

Find the words.

A	N	D	O	X	I	N	M	O	F	G
O	J	O	G	G	I	N	G	R	O	T
L	I	T	F	A	H	C	S	T	F	O
T	K	N	O	S	S	T	I	R	F	Y
E	O	F	F	I	T	R	U	E	B	Y
N	F	C	H	E	S	S	U	A	A	B
N	C	K	O	L	S	Y	O	D	B	A
I	I	S	L	O	P	O	R	I	F	O
S	T	M	U	S	I	C	T	N	B	Y
T	I	F	F	I	R	G	A	G	C	U
F	O	O	T	B	A	L	L	N	F	O

MAN: MY WIFE THINKS I'M MAD, JUST BECAUSE I LIKE PANCAKES!

DOCTOR: THAT'S QUITE NORMAL. I LIKE PANCAKES, TOO.

MAN: REALLY? YOU MUST COME AND SEE MY COLLECTION SOME TIME!

Going Out

UNIT 6

1 The surprise visit

Cross out the wrong words.

Hello? Is **anyone – someone** at home?
There's **nobody – nowhere** in.
Wait, I can see **anybody – somebody** downstairs.
Where? I can't see **anyone – someone**.

George, I can hear **anything – something**!
Anyone's – someone's at the front door!

Well, I can't hear **anything – something.**

Listen. Oh no! It's your friends – and they're drunk! I don't want them here!

We've got **nothing – noone** in the house. No drinks, no food, **anything – nothing**. And anyway, I don't want to see **anyone – somebody**. I'm tired.

Let's not answer the door. Can you hear **anything – anywhere** now? No, I think they've gone.

Let's go **somewhere – anywhere** else. This is boring!
Do you know **nowhere – anywhere** near here?
No. I don't know **somewhere – anywhere** around here. There's **nowhere – anywhere** we can go now apart from back to the pub!

2 I like – or I'd like?

Put them in.

I'm thirsty. . . . . a drink. Let's go to the pub.

. . . . this restaurant. It's really quiet.

. . . . Indian food. It's so spicy!

Yes, but . . . . Chinese food best of all.

. . . . to go that new bistro in town this evening.

. . . . this sort of place. You just meet so many new people!

. . . . going out on Saturday evenings.

. . . . to ask you round for a meal some time next week.

Oh really? . . . . that very much!

Well, ... cooking Italian food. Is that okay?

3 Plans for the evening

Put the telephone conversation in the right order.

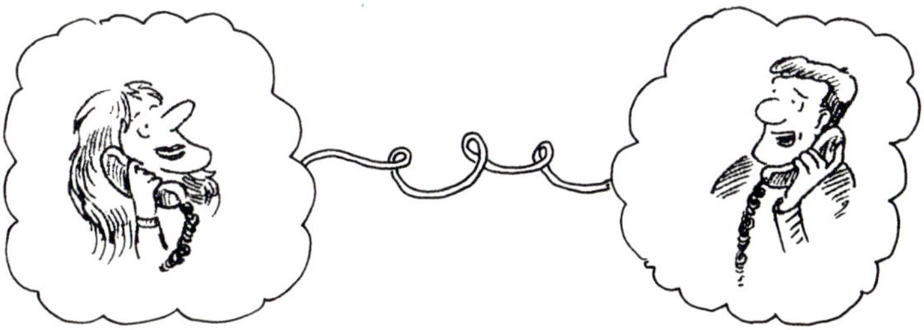

Barry: Hello, Liz. It's Barry here.
Liz: Oh, hi Barry!

Barry: you evening to go would out like this?

. . . .

Liz: would yes, oh, I . a idea great that's.

. . . .

Barry: cinema like you to would to the go?

. . . .

Liz: really not . really cinema like I going to don't the.

. . . .

Barry: like would what to you do?

. . . .

Liz: meal about what a?

. . . .

Barry: idea good ! you restaurant to like the new try Indian would?

. . . .

Liz: that yes, I'd oh like . I curry love !

. . . .

Barry: there eight meet at let's .

. . . .

Liz: Fine. later you see !

. . . .

4 The phone call

Write in the questions with ***would you/do you like****.*

Hello, Alice, it's Frank here.
Oh, hi.

. . . . ?
Go out with you this evening? Yes, I'd love to.

. . . . ?
To the Italian restaurant? Well, actually, I can't. My mother is here until 8.

. . . . ?
Yes, I do. I love dancing.

. . . . ?

The disco? Yes, I would. That's a good idea.

. . . . ?

The one in King Street? Yes, I like that one. They have good music there.

. . . . ?

A lift there? Yes, I would. My mother needs the car.

Great. I'll pick you up about 9 o'clock. Okay?

Fine. See you later.

5 The right way of saying it

Which is right?

1 **Would you like a glass of wine?**
Yes, I'd.
Yes, please.
Yes.

2 **Would you like a sandwich?**
No, thanks.
No, I don't.
No, I wouldn't.

3 **Do you like dancing?**
Yes, I like.
Yes, I love it.
Yes, I would.

4 **Would you like to go out to the Spanish restaurant?**
No.
Actually, I don't really like Spanish food.
No, I wouldn't.

5 **Do you go dancing?**
Do you like dancing?
Would you like a dance?
Yes, okay.

6 The Crown and Anchor

Read the advertisement and answer the questions.

> **The Crown and Anchor**
>
> Toringham Farm Road, Toringham
>
> Come to our beautiful country pub in the heart of the countryside. Try our wonderful traditional English meals and a variety of international dishes in our 18th century dining room. We also have a large selection of British and foreign beers and lagers. Enjoy our open fire in winter or sit in our shady beer garden in summer. There is also a playground for children, and they are welcome in our dining room.
>
> Every Saturday night is folk music night!
>
> Liz and Graham Tailor look forward to your visit.
>
> Open 11 am–11 pm
>
> Lunch from 12.00–3.00

Right or Wrong?

1 The Crown and Anchor is a city pub. . . . .

2 You can get food there. . . . .

3 You can get hot meals all day. . . . .

4 They only have foreign food. . . . .

5 It has got an old dining room. . . . .

6 You can sit outside in summer. . . . .

7 You can't take children there. . . . .

8 There is a disco every week. . . . .

7 At the pub

Underline the odd one out.

1 orange juice pint of bitter lemonade bitter lemon

2 cigarette pipe cigar box of matches

3 whisky mineral water gin lager

4 peanuts packets of crisps ashtray sandwiches

5 barman bar table stool

8 Friends

Put in the right words.

at (x 3) in (x 2) out on back for to

1 Would you like to come . . . . a meal next week?

2 There's a party . . . . John's place on Saturday.

3 Can we meet . . . . the pub this evening?

4 Do you like going . . . . discos?

5 Let's meet . . . . 7.30.

6 There's a good restaurant . . . . Park Street.

7 I can take you . . . . home after the party.

8 This is my house here. Would you like to come . . . . for a coffee?

9 I can't go . . . . this evening. Sorry!

10 There's a good film . . . . at the Rio cinema next month.

9 Sounds

Put the words under the headings.

glass back happy beermat hat half bar flat party ask

æ	ɑː
black	**car**
. . . .	. . . .
. . . .	. . . .
. . . .	. . . .
. . . .	. . . .
. . . .	. . . .
. . . .	. . . .

10 Opposites

What are the opposites of these words?
Use: un-, im-, in-.

happy – *unhappy*
possible – . . . .
able – . . . .
friendly – . . . .
usual – . . . .
polite – . . . .
interesting – . . . .
efficient – . . . .
expensive – . . . .
comfortable – . . . .
personal – . . . .
realistic – . . . .

11 Look, see, and watch

Put in the right words.

1 . . . . over there – there's a new restaurant.

2 I'd like to . . . . TV this evening.

3 I want to . . . . the sights in the city tomorrow.

4 . . . . at this photo. You can . . . . Jim at the party!

5 That waiter over there . . . . very unfriendly!

6 Let me . . . . at the newspaper.

7 . . . . you at 6 o'clock then!

8 He sits in the park and . . . . the children playing.

9 That girl is . . . . over here at us!

10 I'll . . . . you at the pub.

12 Puzzle: At the pub

What are the jumbled words?

1 goeran ueijc . . . .

2 atwre . . . .

3 ebre . . . .

4 tritbe enmlo . . . .

5 meldeona . . . .

6 syiwkh . . . .

UNIT 7 Daily Bread

1 At the corner shop

Put the dialogue in the right order.

1 Goodbye
2 Yes, I'd like a jar of instant coffee, too, please.
3 Just a moment, I'll get one. Here you are, sir.
4 Thank you. And here's your change. Goodbye.
5 Certainly, sir. How many would you like?
6 £3.43
7 They're 30p each. Would you like anything else?
8 Hello. I'd like some apples, please.
9 Thanks. That's all then. How much is that altogether?
10 Four, please. How much are they?
11 £3.43? Here you are.
12 Good morning, can I help you?

2 Money, money, money

How much money is there?

1

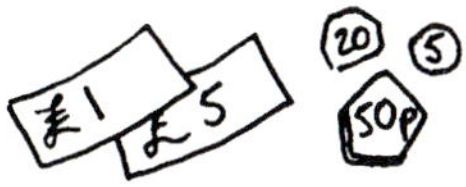

2

3

4

1 £ . . . .

2 £ . . . .

3 £ . . . .

4 £ . . . .

3 Shopping lists

How much is it altogether?

1 butter
1 lb onions
6 apples
newspaper

2 cornflakes
chocolate
eggs
beefburgers
jam

3 2 pears
toilet paper
cheese
bread
lemonade

1 £ . . . . 2 £ . . . . 3 £ . . . .

4 How much or how many?

Put the right one in.

1 .... pears would you like?

2 .... money have you got?

3 .... sugar do we need?

4 .... postcards do you want?

5 .... meat do you need?

6 .... bottles of milk shall I get?

7 .... beer do you want me to buy?

8 .... sausages do we want?

5 Different things

Compare the items.

1 These bananas (cheap) . . . . those ones.
2 This meat (fresh) . . . . that.
3 This coffee (expensive) . . . . that one.
4 This bacon (salty) . . . . the other one.
5 This curry powder (hot) . . . . the other sorts.
6 I find this magazine (interesting) . . . . that one.
7 This tea is much (good) . . . . the other sort.
8 These apples look (nice) . . . . those others.
9 The small packets (bad) . . . . value than the large ones.
10 Their pineapples (big) . . . . the ones in the supermarket.

6 A shopping scene

Complete the dialogue.

Shopkeeper: Good morning. Can I help you?

Customer: . . . .
Shopkeeper: A jar of jam? What sort would you like?

Customer: . . . .
Shopkeeper: Strawberry jam? Here you are. Anything else for you?

Customer: . . . .
Shopkeeper: A kilo of potatoes? Just a moment. Here you are.

Customer: . . . .
Shopkeeper: How much altogether? That's £1.60.

Customer Here you are. Thank you. Goodbye.
Shopkeeper: Thank you. 'bye.

7 Sunday

Read the article and answer the questions.

Sunday, lovely Sunday!

I love Sundays! I walk to the local newsagent's and buy my Sunday newspaper, have a chat to Ranjit, the Pakistani shopkeeper, and then it's back home for breakfast. I always have a cooked breakfast – the good old, traditional, Great British Breakfast! Bacon, eggs, fried bread, and toast and marmalade afterwards. And, of course, a big pot of tea. I take my time reading the newspapers, and then it's time to get the …

True or false?

		T	F
1	The writer buys his newspaper after breakfast.	■	■
2	The shopkeeper is from India.	■	■
3	He talks to the shopkeeper for a while.	■	■
4	He has something typically British for breakfast.	■	■
5	He has toast and marmalade first, then the cooked breakfast.	■	■
6	He reads his newspaper quickly.	■	■

8 Shopping. The right way to do it

Which one is right?

1 *You go into a shop. What can you say?*
How do you do?
Hi!
Hello.

2 *You would like to buy a kilo of tomatoes. What can you say?*
Give me a kilo of tomatoes.
I'd like a kilo of tomatoes, please.
I want a kilo of tomatoes.

3 *Now you want to buy a grapefruit. What can you say?*
I'd like a grapefruit, too, please.
I become a grapefruit, please.
I get a grapefruit, please.

4 *You want to know how much a lettuce costs. What can you say?*
What costs a lettuce?
How much does a lettuce cost?
How much money is a lettuce?

5 *You want to know how much it all costs. What can you say?*
What does that make?
How much is that altogether?
What is the cost of it all?

6 *You want to pay. Do you . . .*
. . . put the money on the counter?
. . . put the money in the shopkeeper's hand?
. . . put the money into the cash register?

7 *When you give the shopkeeper the money, what can you say?*
Here you are.
Keep the change.
Please.
There's your money.

9 Shopping items

Which go together? Some have got more than one answer.

jar	cola	tube	chocolate
packet	bread	roll	milk
box	crisps	bag	cornflakes
bottle	toilet paper	bar	toothpaste
tin	biscuits	loaf	soap
can	jam		matches
			baked beans

a jar of jam ....

....

....

....

....

....

....

10 Shops

Where can you get the things?
Order the items under the right headings.

cosmetics bread meat toiletries cake sausages magazines medicine newspapers rolls cigarettes

newsagent's	baker's	chemist's/drugstore	butcher's
....	....	....	....
....	....	....	....
....	....	....	....

11 Food

What are they?

1 cheese, cream, butter, milk are all **milk products**.

2 cauliflower, leek, onion, potato are all . . . .

3 beef, pork, lamb, veal are all . . . .

4 orange, banana, pineapple, cherry are all . . . .

12 Sounds

Order the words under the headings.

sir where burn pair here wear near turn pear clear hear fair

eə	ɪə	ɜː
chair	dear	her
. . . .	. . . .	. . . .
. . . .	. . . .	. . . .
. . . .	. . . .	. . . .
. . . .	. . . .	. . . .

13 Making words *-able* or *-ible*?

Put in the right endings to the words.

1 You can wash this. It's wash**able**.

2 Be careful. That's break . . . .

3 You can eat that. It's ed . . . .

4 It was a very enjoy . . . . meal.

5 You can throw this away. It's dispos . . . .

6 You can see it from here. It's vis . . . .

14 Crossword

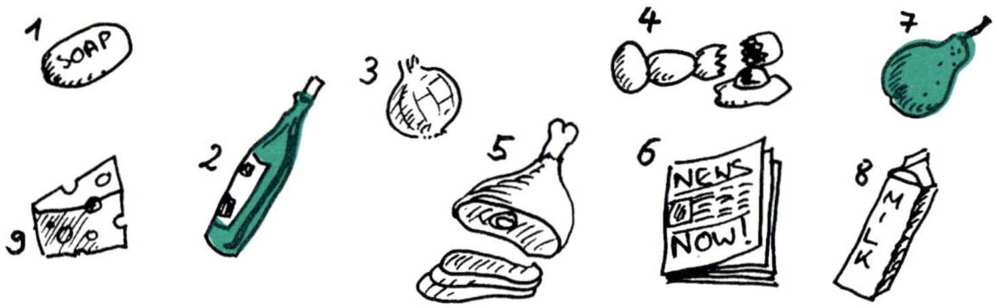

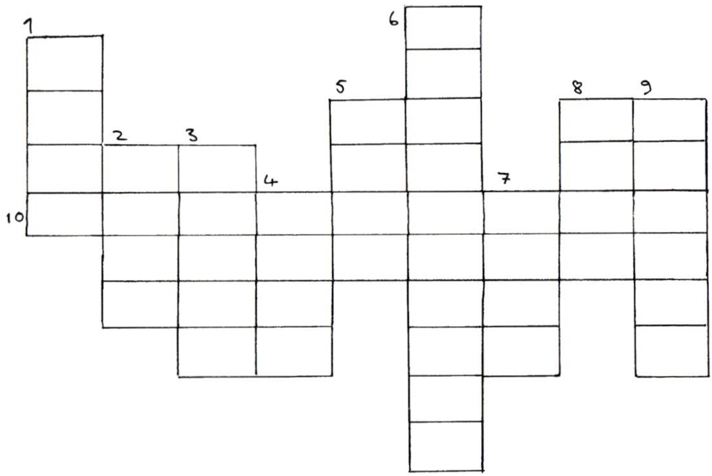

Stores and Floors

UNIT 8

1 *much* or *many*?

Put in the right one.

1 How . . . . money have you got on you?

2 How . . . . stamps do we need?

3 We haven't got . . . . bread at home.

4 They don't sell . . . . of these coats at this time of year.

5 I don't do . . . . shopping at that department store.

6 I never have . . . . time, so I go to the supermarket round the corner.

2 The post office

Put the sentences together.

1 Can I help you?
2 How much is that altogether?
3 Six first class stamps please.
4 Can you change this £20 note, please?
5 Can I send a fax from here?
6 I'd like to send this parcel to Germany.

a Just a moment. That's £2.50.
b Germany? Just a moment. I'll weigh it.
c Yes. I'd like two stamps for these letters, please.
d Certainly. Here you are.
e Yes, sure. How would you like it? A ten and two fives?
f Yes, you can.

3 The jacket

Put in the right superlatives.

SPECIAL OFFER: STORM-TEX JACKETS!!!

It's the . . . . (late) thing in rainwear! Our new STORM-TEX jackets are the . . . . (good) protection against the . . . . (bad) sort of weather. 100% STORM-TEX, our jackets have the . . . . (comfortable) cotton lining, and are the . . . . (light) of their kind on the market today! AND they are the . . . . expensive! We have the . . . . (large) range of the . . . . (fashionable) colours.

Find them in our Clothes Department. We also have the . . . . (big) selection of autumn clothing in town.

4 The Menswear Department

*Put in **one** or **ones**.*

Man: What do you think of this tie?

Woman: It's awful! I prefer this green . . . . here.

Man: I don't like it. Look at those . . . . over there.

What about this brown . . . .?

Woman: Yes, that's the nicest . . . . here. Now. You need new socks. What do you think of these

blue . . . .?

Man: They're all right. These brown . . . . are nicer, though.

Woman: Brown! Always brown! Why don't you take these

. . . .?

Man: Red! You're joking! Oh, look at that jacket over there.

Woman: Where? You mean that grey . . . .?

Man: No! The . . . . with the stripes.

Woman: Oh, I don't like that . . . . at all. Why don't you wear some bright colours?

Always boring, dark . . . .!

5 A helpful assistant

Put in the right words.

at the bottom   **downstairs**   **behind**   **on** (x 3)
between   **through**   **next to**

Excuse me, where's the children's department, please?

It's . . . . the second floor, ... the cafeteria.
Oh, yes. And where are the special offers on underpants?

Over there, ... the trousers and the jeans.
Where? I can't see them.
No, you can't because the shelves are in front of them.

They're . . . . the shelves.

What's that pile with the sign . . . . the top?
Socks. They're also a special offer.

I don't like looking . . . . piles of socks! The good ones are

always . . . . of the pile! Where is the sports department?

Sports!? . . . . the first floor.
And the exit?

. . . ., sir.

6 The department store

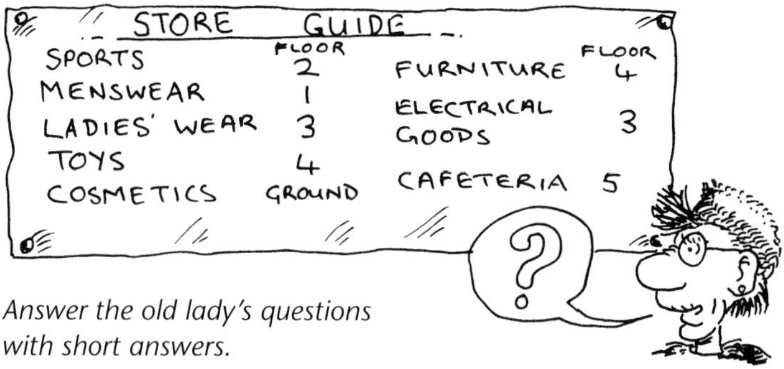

Answer the old lady's questions with short answers.

1 Where can I find a football?

In the sports department on the . . . . floor.

. . . .

2 Where's the cafeteria?

. . . .

3 I'm looking for a pair of jeans for my son. Where can I find them?

. . . .

4 I want to buy some perfume. Where can I find some?

. . . .

5 Where do I find chairs?

. . . .

6 Where can I get a skirt for myself?

. . . .

7 I want to buy a lamp. Where can I go?

To . . . .

8 I'm looking for a teddy bear. Where must I go?

To . . . .

7 Clothes

Write in the names of the clothes.

8 *-ful* or *-less*?

Put the right forms of the words into the sentences.

1 It's **hopeless**. I can't find anything to fit! **(hope)**

2 What a . . . . coat! **(beauty)**

3 It's a quiet shop. It's very . . . . **(peace)**

4 Look at that assistant! He's dropping everything!
He's really . . . .! **(care)**

5 Their range of ties is . . . .! **(end)**

6 These shirts are lively and . . . .! **(colour)**

7 What a nice man. He's very . . . . **(help)**

8 This is very good. It's really . . . . **(use)**

9 This is no good at all! It's . . . .! **(use)**

10 I don't know what to say! I'm . . . .! **(speech)**

11 What a lovely little dog! It's really . . . .! **(play)**

12 That dog is friendly. He's . . . . **(harm)**

9 Opposites

Write down the opposites.

loose large ugly uncomfortable dark short untidy colourless soft narrow

colourful . . . .

smart . . . .

beautiful . . . .

small . . . .

wide . . . .

long . . . .

tight . . . .

rough . . . .

bright . . . .

comfortable . . . .

10 Sounds

Put the words under the headings.

women key canteen sit eat system lift cheap scene little field fifty

ɪ	iː
fit	**feet**
. . . .	. . . .
. . . .	. . . .
. . . .	. . . .
. . . .	. . . .
. . . .	. . . .
. . . .	. . . .

11 "wie"

*What's the right translation of "**wie**" in these sentences?*

what (x 2) **like** (x 2) **as** **how**

1 Wie alt bist du?

. . . . old are you?

2 Diese Krawatte ist nicht so schön wie die andere.

This tie isn't as nice . . . . the other one.

3 Wie wäre es mit diesem Hemd?

. . . . about this shirt?

4 Ich möchte einen Mantel wie deinen.

I want a coat . . . . yours.

5 Der Hut schaut aus wie ein Helm!

The hat looks . . . . a helmet!

6 Wie heißen Sie?

. . . . is your name?

12 Puzzle: clothes

P	S	H	I	R	T	C	K
L	F	U	S	H	O	E	S
T	R	O	U	S	E	R	S
D	O	S	O	C	K	S	T
R	S	K	I	R	T	U	I
E	F	F	Y	O	B	A	E
S	J	A	C	K	E	T	A
S	S	T	R	D	S	F	O

UNIT 9 Eating Out

1 At the restaurant

Put the dialogue in the right order.

1 Waiter: How would you like your steak, sir?
2 Man: A pint of lager for me please. What about you, Sarah?
3 Waiter: Tomato soup, sir.
4 Waiter: Are you ready to order?
5 Waiter: What would you like to drink with your meal?
6 Woman: I'd like a glass of dry white wine.
7 Man: Medium, please. What are you having, Sarah?
8 Woman: I'd like a shrimp cocktail, followed by the steak and kidney pie.
9 Man: Yes, we are. What's the soup of the day?
10 Man: Okay. I'll have the soup, and then I'd like the fillet steak with chips and salad.

The right order is . . . .

2 The meal

What do they order?

Jim: Now, let me see. I'll have a soup of the day, please.
Bob: Me too. Oh, wait a minute. What *is* the soup today?
Waiter: Cream of mushroom, sir.
Jim: Oh, I don't like mushrooms. I'll have a shrimp cocktail instead.
Bob: Oh, yes. Me, too.
Waiter: And do you still want the soup, sir?
Bob: No, thanks. Just the shrimp cocktail.
Waiter: And to follow?
Bob: I'd like the vegetable casserole, please.
Jim: And I'll have the grilled plaice.
Bob: Is there garlic in the casserole?
Waiter: Yes, sir.
Bob: Well, I'll have a fillet steak instead please. With potatoes. Oh, no, with chips, please.
Waiter: What vegetables would you like with your steak, sir?
Bob: Peas, please.
Jim: And I'll have peas and boiled potatoes with my fish.
Bob: Er, can I change that? I'd prefer a green salad. No peas. Sorry!

Waiter: And to drink?
Bob: A half of lager – no, a pint, please.
Jim: And I'd like a glass of red wine.
Bob: With fish?
Jim: Oh, you're right. I'll have white wine. A glass of dry white wine.

		Bob	Jim
1	cream of mushroom soup		
2	shrimp cocktail		
3	vegetable casserole		
4	grilled plaice		
5	fillet steak		
6	boiled potatoes		
7	chips		
8	peas		
9	green salad		
10	half of lager		
11	pint of lager		
12	glass of red wine		
13	glass of white wine		

3 The bill

Cross out the wrong words.

Waiter, can I **get** – **have** the bill, please.
Certainly, sir. **Just** – **In** a moment, sir.
Oh, can I pay **with** – **by** cheque?
Sorry, sir we only **want** – **take** credit cards.
Okay. Here **you are** – **is it**.
Will – **Could** you sign here, please?
Okay.
Here is your card and your **recipe** – **receipt**, sir.

4 Help

*What are they saying? Put in **I'd** or **I'll**.*

1 I haven't got a fork!

. . . . get you one, sir.

2 What will you have, sir?

. . . . like the steak, please.

3 I haven't got any money on me!

That's okay. . . . . pay.

4 What's in the casserole?

I don't know. . . . . ask the waiter.

5 Would you like a starter, madam?

Yes, please. . . . . like a soup.

6 I can't open this bottle

Give it to me . . . . try.

5 A hungry man

Put in the right words.

off	**under**	**on** (x 2)	**to**	**in**	**with**	**up**	**at** (x 2)

"Look . . . . that man over there! The one . . . . the table . . . . the corner. He has got two really big steaks . . . . his plate and the waiter is going . . . . his table . . . . a large plate of chips! There's a full bottle of wine . . . . his table and an empty one . . . . the table by his feet! I don't believe it! I'm sure he can't stand . . . . . . ! He'll probably fall . . . . his chair!"

6 The right way to say it

What's right?

1 Can I have the card, please?
Can I have the menu, please?
I'll have the menu, please.
2 Can I have some bread, please?
Can I have a bread, please?
3 I'll have the apple pea, please.
I'll have the apple pie, please.
4 Waiter!
Here!
Please!
5 Would you like a starter, sir?
No, I wouldn't.
Thank you.
No, thanks.
6 A glass of wine for my woman, please.
A glass of wine for my wife, please.
7 I'd like a dessert, please.
I'd like a desert, please.
8 Pay!
Pay, please.
Can I have the bill, please?

7 Fish and chips

Read the text and answer the questions.

The Chippie

In the High Street, among the Indian restaurants, the Chinese restaurants, the pizza places and pubs, the burger bars, kebab take-aways, bistros and sandwich bars you can find the traditional British fast food place: the fish and chip shop. "The chippie", as it is often known, sells more or less the same things all over the country: fish and chips. Of course you can have different sorts of fish: cod and chips, plaice and chips, haddock and chips, and other specialities: sausage and chips, pie and chips. Obviously the quality varies – from the crispy delicious battered fish to the greasy overcooked fish with "soggy" chips. Salt and malt vinegar are usually put on the food, too. No plates here – the fish and chips are wrapped in paper to take away. A very popular meal in Britain – especially on a Friday and Saturday night.

True or false?

	T	F
1 You can often find a lot of places to eat in a town's High Street.		
2 Haddock, cod, and plaice are sorts of meat.		
3 Fish and chip shops only sell fish and chips.		
4 The quality is always very good.		
5 Some people put malt vinegar on their fish and chips.		
6 You get your fish and chips on a plate.		
7 A lot of people in Britain like fish and chips.		
8 People like fish and chips for breakfast.		

8 Making words: *under-* and *over-*

Make words with **under**- *or* **over**-.

1 I'll just have a salad. I'm a bit **over**weight at the moment.

2 These vegetables are too hard. They're . . . . cooked.

3 It's an expensive restaurant. Their food is . . . . priced.

4 That bill can't be right. I think the waiter . . . . charged us.

5 That waitress is so busy. She's . . . . worked.

6 She's probably . . . . paid, though. Waitresses don't earn very much.

7 This meat's black! It's . . . . done.

9 At the restaurant table

Write in the words.

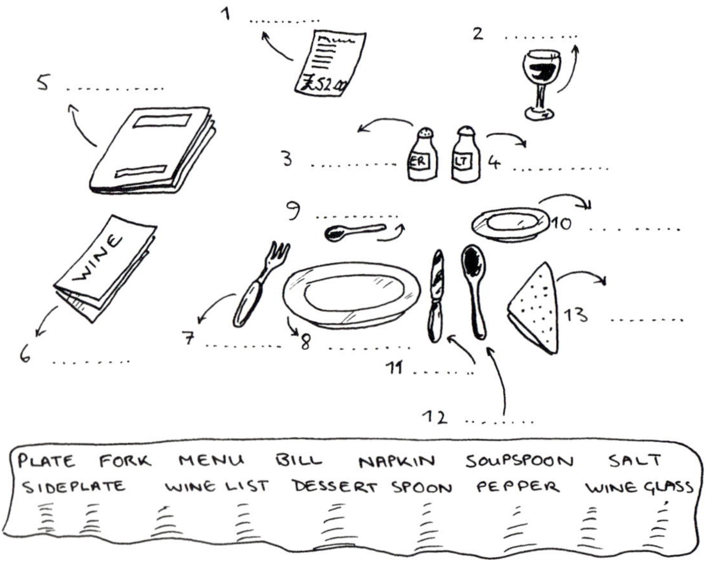

10 Talking about food

Put in the right words.

tender tasty awful burnt salty bland delicious tough sweet hot (spicy)

1 This fish is really good! It's . . . .!

2 My casserole isn't very good. Actually, it's . . . .!

3 Look at this chicken – it's overdone! It's . . . .!

4 This meat's like an old shoe! It's really . . . .!

5 My steak is great. It's not at all tough. It's . . . .!

6 There's too much salt in this! It's really . . . .!

7 There's a lot of chilli in this. It's rather . . . .!

8 This tastes of nothing! It's really . . . .!

9 There's too much sugar in this pie. It's very . . . .

10 This tastes good. Is yours as . . . .?

11 Sounds

Which is the odd word out?

1 ɔː
fork talk table pork call sort ball

Odd word out: . . . .

2 eɪ
wait walk plate table late sale

Odd word out: . . . .

12 Restaurant words

What are the words?

_ e _ _ ert ....

b _ _ l ....

_ e _ u ....

_ ni _ e ....

_ la _ e ....

f _ r _ ....

s _ ea _ ....

_ a _ ter ....

Away from Home

UNIT 10

1 Asking the way

Write in the names of the places and roads you read about in the right spaces.

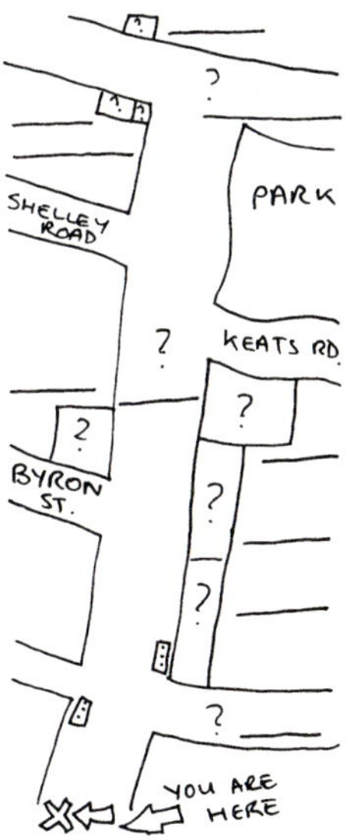

"Excuse me, where is the post office?"
"The post office? Let me see. Go down here, the High Street, and cross over Milton Road, at the traffic lights. Go straight on, past the bank on your right, and then past the café and you'll see a big record shop on the corner.
There's a supermarket on the other side of the High Street, too. Cross the road, that's Keats Road, and go past the park on the right. Cross the road – the High Street – and you'll see a fish and chip shop on the corner. Turn left into Park Road and the post office is next to the fish and chip shop, opposite a chemist's."

2 Stranger in town

Put the two halves of the sentences together.

1 Excuse me, can you	a) the nearest bank?
2 Excuse me, is there	b) where the police station is?
3 Excuse me, do you know	c) any telephones near here?
4 Excuse me, where	d) a supermarket near here?
5 Excuse me, where's	e) tell me the way to the bank?
6 Excuse me, are there	f) is the fish and chip shop?

1 . . . . . 2 . . . . . 3 . . . . . 4 . . . . . 5 . . . . . 6 . . . .

3 How to get there

Put in the right words.

Turn left into   Take the second turning   Go straight on   Go down   Cross the road

1 . . . .

2 . . . .

3 . . . .

4 . . . .

5 . . . .

1

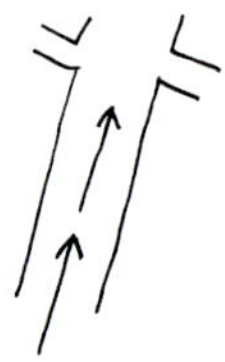

2

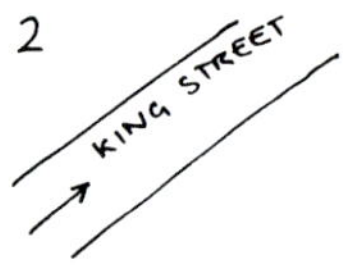

3

4

5

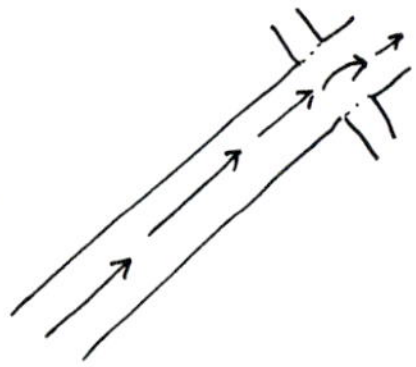

4 Where is the café?

between the florist's and the bank near the bank on the corner next to the bank opposite the bank

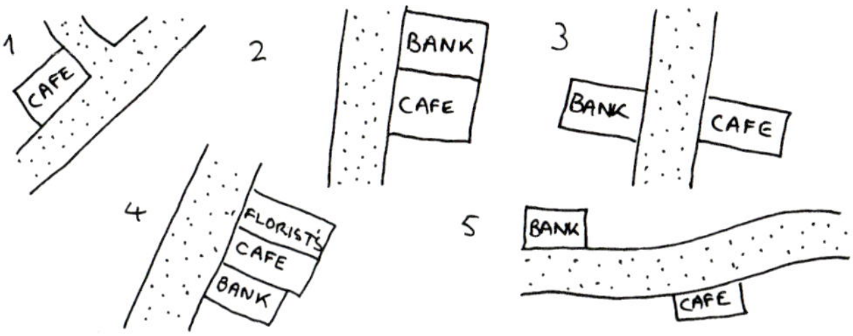

1 . . . .

2 . . . .

3 . . . .

4 . . . .

5 . . . .

5 At the hotel reception

Complete the dialogue with the phrases below.

Could I have your name, please? With a bath or a shower? When is it for? I'd like to book Would you like a single room or a double room? How much is the room? Can I help you? Does that include breakfast?

Good morning. Marina hotel. . . . .?

Good morning. . . . . a room, please.

. . . .?

It's for next Friday and Saturday – the 3rd and 4th.

. . . . ?

A double room, please.

. . . . ?

With a shower. . . . . ?

It's £80 a night.

. . . . ?

Yes, it does. . . . . ?

It's Martin, Mr and Mrs Martin.
Thank you, Mrs Martin.

6 The hotel manager

Put in the right form of the verbs.

Give me the key, please. (give)
Don't be rude to the guests! (not – be)

1 . . . . the guests their room. (show)

2 . . . . the luggage up to their room. (take)

3 . . . . that suitcase! (not – drop)

4 . . . . late again! (not – be)

5 . . . . careful! (be)

6 . . . . back to work! (get)

7 . . . . smoking! (stop)

8 . . . . in the kitchen! (not – smoke)

7 The bad fax

What are the missing words?

at   to   with   for   on (x 2)   of   in

I'd like to book a single room . . . . three nights. I'll be arriving . . . . Friday, probably . . . . the afternoon. I've stayed . . . . your hotel before, and I'd like to have the same room if possible. I can't remember the room number, but it's . . . . the top floor . . . . a beautiful view . . . . the city. Please confirm my booking by fax . . . . the address above.

8 Bed and Breakfast

Read the text and answer the questions.

Mrs B's B+B

Come to Mrs B's B+B for a Beautiful stay!

We have two lovely rooms overlooking the garden, one double room and one single room – ideal for a family. We serve either a cooked English breakfast, or, if you prefer, a continental breakfast. Evening meals are served if booked in advance.

We're – cheaper than any hotel!
– close to the city centre.
– near the park.
– only 10 minutes drive from the coast.

Mrs Bryant, her husband Jim and their dog Toto look forward to your visit.

True or false?	T	F
1 B+B means "beautiful breakfast".		
2 They have two double rooms.		
3 You can have a cooked or continental breakfast.		
4 Hotels are more expensive.		
5 They are a long way from the city centre.		
6 You can see their garden from the bedrooms.		
7 Mrs Bryant is married.		
8 They haven't got a pet.		

9 The right way to say it

What's right?

1 Where's the park?
Excuse me, can you tell me where the park is?
Please, where is the park?

2 Excuse me, is there a bank in the near?
Excuse me, is there a bank near here?
Excuse me, is there a bank near by here?

3 Can you say me the way to the post office?
Can you tell to me the way to the post office?
Can you tell me the way to the post office?

4 The butcher's is next to the supermarket.
The butcher's is next the supermarket.

5 The bus stop is in front of the pub.
The bus stop is in front the pub.

6 Thank you very much.
Welcome.
Please.
You're welcome.

10 *next* and *nearest*

Put in the right one.

1 Where is the . . . . post box, please?

2 The . . . . bus is in half an hour.

3 What are your plans for . . . . weekend?

4 What time is the . . . . film?

5 The café . . . . to my house is round the corner in Green Street.

6 The . . . . police station is miles away from here.

7 The supermarket is . . . . to the chemist's.

11 Sounds

Put the words under the headings.

street guide size buy bike feet field try meet arrive scene key

iː	aɪ
eat	**white**
. . . .	. . . .
. . . .	. . . .
. . . .	. . . .
. . . .	. . . .
. . . .	. . . .
. . . .	. . . .

12 Making words: *-ess* or *-woman*?

Make words with the right endings.

1 She works in a restaurant. She's a waitr. . . . .

2 She runs the hotel. She's the manager . . . .

3 She's won the race! What a great sports . . . . !

4 Of course she can speak French – she's a French . . . .

5 She works in that shop. She's a sales . . . .

6 She's got a job on a plane as a steward . . . .

7 I know her from that film on TV. She an actr . . . .

8 She works for the police. She's a police . . . .

13 Crossword: At the hotel

CLUES

1 . . . . is from 6.00 am to 10.00 am.

2 You check in at the . . . .

3 Your room is on the first . . . .

4 Do you want a room with a bath or a . . . . ?

5 You can take the . . . . to the top floor.

6 I want to speak to the hotel . . . . !

7 Your room is number five, and here is your . . . .

UNIT 11 Up and Away

1 The holiday

Put in the right forms of ***was/wasn't, were/weren't.***

"It . . . . so wonderful! We . . . . in a really modern hotel with a swimming pool, but there . . . . any people in it because the beach . . . . so beautiful. I . . . . in the water very much because I can't swim very well, but the children . . . . in and out of the sea all day! The food . . . . delicious, and those waiters! Well, they . . . . charming and very good-looking! Tom . . . . very well on the last day. In fact, we . . . . all a little bit ill for a while. It . . . . too hot. Anyway, what . . . . your holiday in Clacton like?"

2 Back from abroad

Answer the questions with short answers.

1 Was the food good?

Yes, ...

2 Were the hotel guests friendly?

Yes, ...

3 Was the sea clean?

Yes, ...

4 Were the people friendly?

No, ... Not really, I'm afraid.

5 Were the children happy?

Yes, ...

6 Was the hotel modern?

No, ... It was quite old, but nice.

7 Were the sights interesting?

No, ... There wasn't anything to see.

8 Were you and your husband satisfied with the holiday?

Yes, ...

9 Was Sarah good?

Yes, ...

10 Was your husband in the water at all?

No, ... He's afraid of the sea!

3 Back from abroad

Put in the questions with the right question word.

where	**how much**	**who**	**what**	**how**	**how many**
why	**when**				

1 . . . . the weather like?
The weather wasn't very good.

2 . . . . the hotel?
The hotel was a bit noisy.

3 . . . . it so loud?
Because there was a disco next door.

4 . . . . the hotel?
It was quite a long way from the coast.

5 . . . . your hired car?
It was very expensive!

6 . . . . people . . . . on the beach?
There were hundreds of them. It was awful!

7 . . . . at the famous castle?
We were there on the second day.

8 . . . . . there to meet you at the airport when you got back?
Tony picked us up in his car.

4 On holiday

Put in the right verbs in the simple past.

watch play look talk walk check arrive show be (x 2)

Dear Pete,

Here's a short letter from sunny Spain! We . . . . this morning at 10 o'clock and . . . . in at the hotel. What a place! At first I thought it . . . . like a prison! I like it now, though. The people at the hotel . . . . very friendly, and lunch . . . . delicious! In the afternoon we . . . . down to the beach. I . . . . the waves for a while and then . . . . to some people who were fishing. They . . . . us some of their fish and a giant shell. In the evening we . . . . cards, but we were all so tired. I'm in bed now writing this so I'll finish it tomorrow.

5 The postcard

by under along in (x 2) **to over at** (x 4)

Dear Emma,
Having a lovely time here . . . . the sea-side. Our hotel is right . . . . the coast. We like it . . . . the hotel, but we go . . . . the beach every day. I'm sitting . . . . a deckchair . . . . the beach . . . . the moment. Terry is . . . . the sea all day – he loves it! He spends most of the time . . . . water, looking for fish! In the evening we walk . . . . the beach with the waves . . . . our feet, and the seagulls . . . . our heads. After that we have a drink . . . . the swimming pool. See you soon,
Love from Sammi.

6 Sunny Spain

Read the text and answer the questions.

I wanted to get away from grey old England. Sun, sea, good food in little restaurants and interesting local people. Well, it wasn't like that. Our hotel was full of English people and there was English food on the menu at the hotel restaurant. I walked along the beach to a small village in search of a little restaurant. But when I found one it was full of English tourists eating fish and chips and drinking English beer. Even at the supermarket there were English things – just like in a supermarket back home. The beach was full of English tourists with sunburn. Some of them were already drunk at midday! In the evening I looked in at a disco – yes, you guessed it – full of English people. Where were the Spaniards, the local people? Next year I'll go to the seaside in England and pretend I'm in Spain!

True or false?

	T	F
1 The writer wanted to go abroad.		
2 There was English food at the hotel.		
3 The writer walked to a restaurant in the city.		
4 The supermarket looked like an English one.		
5 The tourists weren't careful about the sun.		
6 There were a lot of Spaniards at the disco.		
7 The writer wants to go on holiday in England next year.		

7 The right way to say it

What's right?

1 I need a sunglasses.
I need a pair of sunglasses.
2 I want to buy a pair of swimming trunks.
I want to buy a swimming trunks.
3 We must get a sun umbrella.
We must get a sunshade.
4 Careful! You've got sunburn!
Carefull! You've got sunfire!
5 It's cool here in the shadow.
It's cool here in the shade.

8 The seaside

What are the words?

beach sand cliff seaweed crab beach towel bucket and spade sand castle sunshade deckchair sea wave shell starfish shore

9 Making words

*Make words with **sun**- and write them under the pictures.*

1 ______________

2 ______________

3 ______________

4 ______________

5 ______________

6 ______________

7 ______________

8 ______________

glasses tan lotion tan shade shine stroke bathe burn

10 Sounds

Put the verbs under the right headings in their simple past form.

play walk visit live work start want look stay arrive hate finish watch show wait

d	t	ɪd
play**ed**	walk**ed**	visit**ed**
....	....	....
....	....	....
....	....	....
....	....	....

11 "vor"

*What is **vor** in English?*

in front of **before** **ago**

1 Vor einer Woche waren wir auf Kreta.

We were in Crete a week . . . .

2 Abends saß er immer vorm Fernseher.

He sat . . . . the TV in the evenings.

3 Wir gingen vor dem Frühstück zum Strand.

We went to the beach . . . . breakfast.

4 Vor einem Jahr waren wir in Italien.

A year . . . . we were in Italy.

5 Wir gingen vorm Sonnenuntergang am Strand entlang.

We walked along the beach . . . . sunset.

12 Puzzle: the seaside

What are the words?

1 _ e a _ h . . . .

2 _ e c _ c _ a _ r . . . .

3 s _ _ g _ _ s _ _ s . . . .

4 _ a v _ . . . .

5 _ _ n s h _ d _ . . . .

6 s _ _ b _ _ n . . . .

The Big City

UNIT 12

1 Verbs

Join the verbs to their simple past forms with a line.

buy	took
eat	was/were
do	met
drink	had
go	bought
take	ate
meet	got
see	drank
speak	did
travel	went
get	saw
have	said
be	travelled
say	spoke

2 A day in the big city

Put in the right form of the verb.

"It . . . . (be) great yesterday. I . . . . (go) to London with Terry. First we . . . . (take) the tube to Oxford Circus and . . . . (look) around the shops and . . . . (do) a bit of shopping. I . . . . (get) a really nice pair of shoes. Then we . . . . (have) a drink at a really busy pub and I . . . . (eat) an awful pie! Terry . . . . (say) his meal . . . . (be) okay, though. We . . . . (meet) a nice couple from Germany in the pub. They . . . . (speak) very good English and . . . . (tell) us that they . . . . (love) this country. Then we . . . . (go) on a sight-seeing tour by bus. We . . . . (see) so many things – all those things you see on postcards! Later we . . . . (find) a really nice Indian restaurant and . . . . (try) a very hot curry. We . . . . (travel) back by bus quite late."

3 In town

Make these sentences negative.

1 I saw the Tower of London.

. . . .

2 We had a late lunch.

. . . .

3 I liked Trafalgar Square.

. . . .

4 I took a lot of photos.

. . . .

5 I bought some souvenirs.

. . . .

6 We found the Science Museum very interesting.

. . . .

7 We went to St. Paul's Cathedral.

. . . .

8 The weather was very good.

. . . .

4 Sightseeing

Answer the questions with short answers.

1 Did you like Regent's Park?

Yes, ...

2 Did you visit the Tower of London?

No, ...

3 Did your husband go with you?

No, ...

4 Did you go on a sightseeing tour?

Yes, ...

5 Was the weather good?

No, ...

6 Did you go to the National Gallery?

No, ...

7 Did the tour bus go to Greenwich?

No, ...

8 Did you do any shopping?

Yes, ...

5 A trip to London

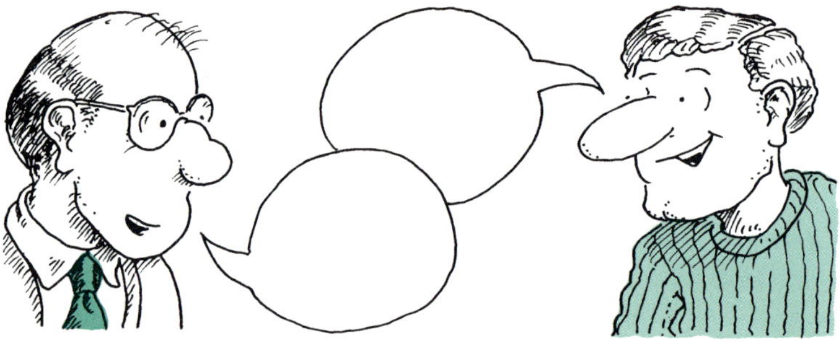

*Write questions with **Did . . .?**.*

1 . . . . London?
Yes, we did. We liked London very much.

2 . . . . shopping?
Yes, we did. We went shopping in the afternoon.

3 . . . . by tube?
Yes, we did. We travelled everywhere by tube.

4 . . . . the British Museum?
No, we didn't. We didn't have time to visit it.

5 .... any speakers at Speaker's Corner?
No, we didn't. We didn't see any speakers there.

6 .... any photos?
Yes, we did. We took hundreds of photos.

7 .... any souvenirs?
Yes, we did. We bought a lot of souvenirs.

8 .... a good day out?
Yes, we did. We had a great day out.

6 A letter from Chinatown

Dear Barry,
Just a short letter to say "hello from Soho!" This place is really interesting – one minute you're walking around London streets full of shops and then you go round the corner and you're in Chinatown. It's full of little Chinese restaurants and shops and Chinese people. You don't hear much English and even the street names are in English and Chinese! It smells so good here – the food, the incense, everything. I went to a wonderful restaurant here and had a really good Chinese meal: Crispy Duck. It was hard to believe I was in the middle of London.

One of these sentences is wrong. Which one?

1 Chinatown is in Soho.
2 Chinatown is in the centre of London.
3 You can eat Chinese food in Chinatown.
4 You can only hear English in Chinatown.
5 Crispy Duck is a Chinese meal.
6 The letter writer likes the smell of the food and incense in Chinatown.

Sentence . . . . is wrong.

7 Around town

Cross out the wrong words.

1 We made a bus tour **around** – **between** the city.
2 I went **straight on** – **along** the river in a boat.
3 We went for a walk **on** – **through** Hyde Park.
4 We had a break at a cafe **between** – **next** Tower Bridge and the Tower of London.
5 They always travel **in** – **on** the underground.
6 I always go **with** – **by** taxi.
7 It's too far go go **by** – **on** foot.
8 I'll meet you **before** – **outside** the tube station.
9 There's a good view of the Thames **from** – **of** the bridge.
10 We walked **over** – **opposite** the bridge to the other side.

8 Pairs

Which words go together?

cinema art gallery river film street map tube postcard bus

1 underground – ....
2 guide – ....
3 boat trip – ....
4 camera – ....
5 souvenir – ....
6 double decker – ....
7 museum – ....
8 theatre – ....

9 Two words to one word

Make words from the two halves.

1 week .... way
2 sight .... step
3 under .... yard
4 time .... table
5 alley .... room
6 super .... ground
7 bath .... side
8 foot .... see
9 church .... market
10 river .... end

10 *make* and *do*

Cross out the wrong ones.

1 That souvenir shop **makes** – **does** a lot of money.
2 This taxi **makes** – **does** a lot of noise!
3 I want to **make** – **do** some shopping in Oxford Street.
4 I think they **made** – **did** a mistake with our change.
5 I **made** – **did** a lot of sightseeing when I was in London.
6 Don't **make** – **do** anything dangerous!
7 He **makes** – **does** his job very well.
8 He **makes** – **does** a living out of the tourist trade.

11 Making words: Nationalities and people

What are their nationalities? The last two letters are always ***-an****.*

Place	**Nationality**
America	....
Russia	....
Brazil	....
Australia	....
Italy	....
Austria	....
Sicily	....
Hungary	....
Chile	....
Europe	....
Canada	....
Morocco	....
Belgium	....
Argentina	....

12 Sounds

Which are the odd ones out? Underline them.

ɔː   bought shout sort

aʊ   out loud four

ɔː   crowd thought caught

aʊ   shower port power

13 Crossword: A trip to the big city

Clues

1 I want to go on a sightseeing . . .
2 I'd like to visit the Tower of . . .
3 What's that book? – It's a . . . to London.
4 Let's go by . . .
5 There's a tourist . . . office.
6 Look! There's a double decker . . .
7 We need a . . . to get into the museum.

What is the word down? . . . .

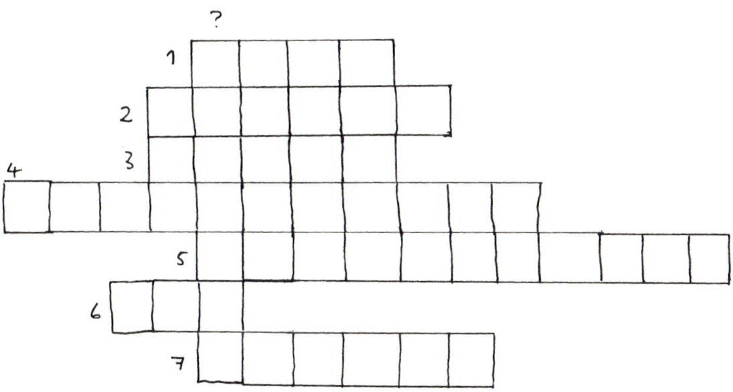

UNIT 13 Last Night . . .

1 Tina's party

Put in the right forms of the verbs.

Jane: Where's Lisa? She . . . . (say) that she . . . . (want) to come this evening.

Kelly: Lisa? When . . . . you . . . . (speak) to her?

Jane: I . . . . (see) her in the High Street yesterday. She . . . . (have) a present for Tina, so I don't know why she isn't here. She . . . . (not – look) ill or anything – she . . . . (look) fine!

Kelly: Well, I . . . . (meet) her in town when I . . . . (buy) this dress, but she . . . . (not – sound) very happy.

Jane: Yes, she and her boyfriend . . . . (break) up a couple of weeks ago. She . . . . (like) him a lot.

Kelly: Tony? Yes, he's good-looking, but he . . . . (not – be) very nice to her. He . . . . (go) out with that other girl at the same time. Terrible.

Jane: Yes, Tony . . . . (try) to kiss me at a disco once.

Kelly: Really! And . . . . he . . . . (get) what he . . . . (want)?

Jane: Kelly! No, he . . . . . . ! I'm not like that!

Kelly: Only joking! Oh. Look. That's Lisa. Who's that man she's with?

2 Last night's party

What are the questions? Put them in with question words.

how long where how many why how when what (x 2) who

1 . . . . the party like?
The party? It was really good.

2 . . . . with?
I went with Lisa.

3 . . . . her?
I met her at a disco.

4 . . . . to the party?
We got to the party a bit late. At about ten o'clock.

5 . . . . late?
We arrived late because I had trouble with the car.

6 . . . . ?
Lisa wore a beautiful red dress. Really sexy!

7 . . . . to the party?
About fifty people came.

8 . . . . go on for?
It went on for about four hours after we arrived – until about two.

9 . . . . home?
We got home by taxi. I didn't want to drive.

3 Disco drama

Put the sentences together.

1 What did you do yesterday?
2 Who went to the disco with you?
3 What happened?
4 How many people helped her?
5 Was Liz okay?
6 Did Jim take her home?
7 So everything was all right in the end?

a Jim and Liz had an argument and Liz fainted!
b Yes, she was. She felt better quite soon.
c No, he didn't until much later. They stayed and danced all evening!
d Jim and Liz, Pete and Di went, too.
e Yes, it was. Jim and Liz are still together!
f None. They all just watched. Well, Pete, Di, Jim and I did, of course.
g I went to the disco.

1 . . . .   2 . . . .   3 . . . .   4 . . . .   5 . . . .   6 . . . .   7 . . . .

4 A holiday romance

Cross out the wrong words.

Dear Angie,
It's fantastic here – there! Everything is better than – as I thought before – for I came here. Guess what? Yes, I'm on – in love! I met him at – into a bar near – near of the beach. – He works there – over here. I looked to – at him, and he always looked to – in my direction. Later he came over – forward and said hello. We talked for – along a while, and he asked me to go for – to a nearby disco with – by him. It was really exciting! We danced together – with us all evening, and then the disco closed. We walked outside – along the beach beneath – below the stars ... The smell of – from the sea, the warm air, the stars! – It was all so romantic! Then, at – on about four o'clock at – in the morning, we walked back to ...

5 The party

☆☆☆☆☆☆☆☆☆☆☆☆☆☆☆☆☆☆

invitation !!!!!

jon and rita would like to invite YOU to their party on saturday 25th march at 8 pm at their place.

bring a friend, a bottle, maybe a salad . . . and a smile!

. . . and don't forget:

it's a BLACK and white fancy dress party!!!!!!!!!!!

☆☆☆☆☆☆☆☆☆☆☆☆☆☆☆☆☆☆

Read the invitation and the letter. Underline the parts of the letter which are wrong.

Last Friday I went to a party at Jon and Tina's friend's house. It started at 7.30 am and was really boring at the beginning. Then guests started to arrive. There were a lot of people because they all brought their parents. They all wore fancy dress in red and black. There was a lot to eat and drink because everybody brought a barrel of beer and some sandwiches.

6 Words together

Put the pairs of words together.

disc	cheque	....
disco	call	....
party	fee	....
admission	pool	....
phone	cream	....
wine	music	....
ice	jockey	....
credit	dress	....
traveller's	card	....
swimming	bar	....

7 Words that sound the same

Cross out the wrong ones.

1 I **hear** – **here** that you come **hear** – **here** every Saturday.
2 That's **there** – **their** car over **their** – **there**.
3 My **two** – **too** friends are here, **two** – **too**.
4 You **knew** – **new** that I was **knew** – **new** here, didn't you?
5 I **read** – **red** that book with the **read** – **red** cover a long time ago.
6 **Our** – **hour** bus comes in half an **our** – **hour**.
7 He likes to smell and **see** – **sea** the **see** – **sea**.
8 My **sun** – **son** lies in the **sun** – **son** all day!
9 Last **weak** – **week** I was ill and I felt very **weak** – **week**.
10 I can't **weight** – **wait** to lose a bit of **weight** – **wait**!

8 *Listen or hear?*

Put the right one in.

1 I always . . . . to music in the evening.

2 I . . . . to a really good play on the radio yesterday.

3 Can you . . . . that strange noise?

4 Can you speak louder, please? I can't . . . . very well.

5 Sorry, I didn't . . . . you at the front door.

6 . . . ., perhaps I can help you with your problem.

7 She never . . . . to me!

8 I . . . . the bad news about Harry last week.

9 If you . . . . carefully, you can . . . . the birds singing.

9 The right way to say it

Which ones are right?

1 How are you?
I'm very fine.
Thank you. Good.
Fine, thanks. And you?

2 That's a very attractive wife over there.
That's a very attractive woman over there.

3 I'd like you to meet my husband.
I'd like you to meet my man.

4 Let me invite you to a drink.
Let me buy you a drink.

5 That man is the colleague of my husband.
That man is my husband's colleague.

6 Look at that tie he's wearing!
Look at that tie he's carrying!

7 There are lots of peoples here.
There are lots or people here.

8 Let's meet us next week.
Let's meet next week.

9 See you next Tuesday!
Same to you!
Yes, see you then.

10 Have a nice evening!
The same!
You, too!

10 Words instead of "not..."

*Rewrite these sentences with **un-**, **im-**, **in-**, **dis-**, **ir-** or **il-**.*

1 Lynn is not happy with her dress.
Lynn is **unhappy** with her dress.

2 I'm afraid Tuesday is not possible for me. Sorry!

I'm afraid Tuesday is . . . . for me. Sorry!

3 I don't like Tina's new boyfriend.

I . . . . Tina's new boyfriend.

4 Well, I don't agree with you. I think he's nice.

Well, I . . . . with you. I think he's nice.

5 I think that good looks are not important.

I think that good looks are . . . .

6 Joan's husband isn't polite to the guests.

Joan's husband is . . . . to the guests.

7 The party on Saturday isn't formal, you know.

The party on Saturday is . . . ., you know.

8 His arguments aren't logical.

His arguments are . . . .

9 It isn't clear to me why he says these things.

It's . . . . to me why he says these things.

10 Careful! These verbs are not regular.

Careful! These verbs are . . . .

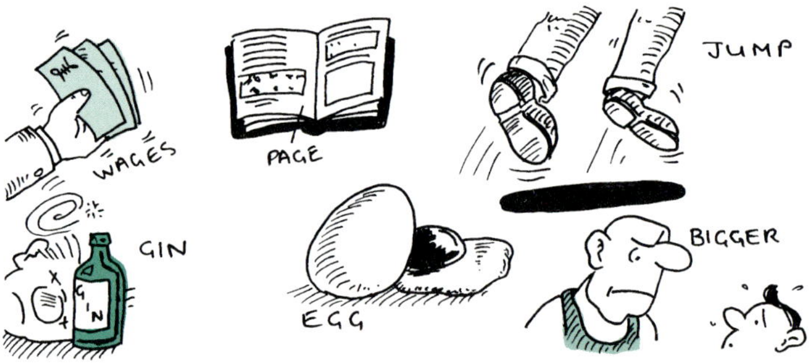

11 Sounds

Which is the odd one out?

dʒ	page	ago	age	. . . .
g	bigger	egg	edge	. . . .
dʒ	wages	gin	guest	. . . .
g	get	jump	garden	. . . .

12 Puzzle: The disco

What are the words?

☆☆☆☆☆☆☆☆☆☆☆☆☆☆☆☆☆☆

1 I thought the **scdi ceyojk** was very good.

2 The **smiuc** was terrible!

3 The **glisht** made me feel strange.

4 There's nothing better than a good **caden**!

☆☆☆☆☆☆☆☆☆☆☆☆☆☆☆☆☆☆

1 .... 2 .... 3 .... 4 ....

UNIT 14 Looking Forward

1 Ready to go

Put the two halves of the sentences together.

1	Tomorrow at this time	a	will be on time.
2	I hope the taxi will come	b	be cold there?
3	I'm sure the taxi	c	I'll phone you.
4	Are you sure	d	we'll be in on the beach.
5	Do you think it will	e	until we are at our hotel.
6	Will we get	f	you won't need a pullover?
7	My cold will be better	g	we get there.
8	I think we'll	h	to pick us up soon.
9	When we arrive	i	when we get to the seaside.
10	I'll probably be tired by the time	j	like it there.
11	I won't phone you	k	to the airport on time?

1 . . . .   2 . . . .   3 . . . .   4 . . . .   5 . . . .   6 . . . .

7 . . . .   8 . . . .   9 . . . .   10 . . . .   11 . . . .

2 The crystal ball

What does the old woman say about the future? Make sentences.

1 You – meet – tall – dark – stranger
"**You will meet a tall, dark stranger.**"

2 You – win – a lot of money – on – lottery

" . . . . "

3 You – live – to be very old

" . . . . "

4 Your – husband – get – very good job

" . . . . "

5 You – not – be ill – this winter

" . . . . "

6 Your daughter – marry – famous actor

" . . . . "

7 Your husband – not – watch football – on TV again

" . . . . "

8 You – move to – luxury villa

" . . . . "

"Yes, but will I be happy?"

3 European weather

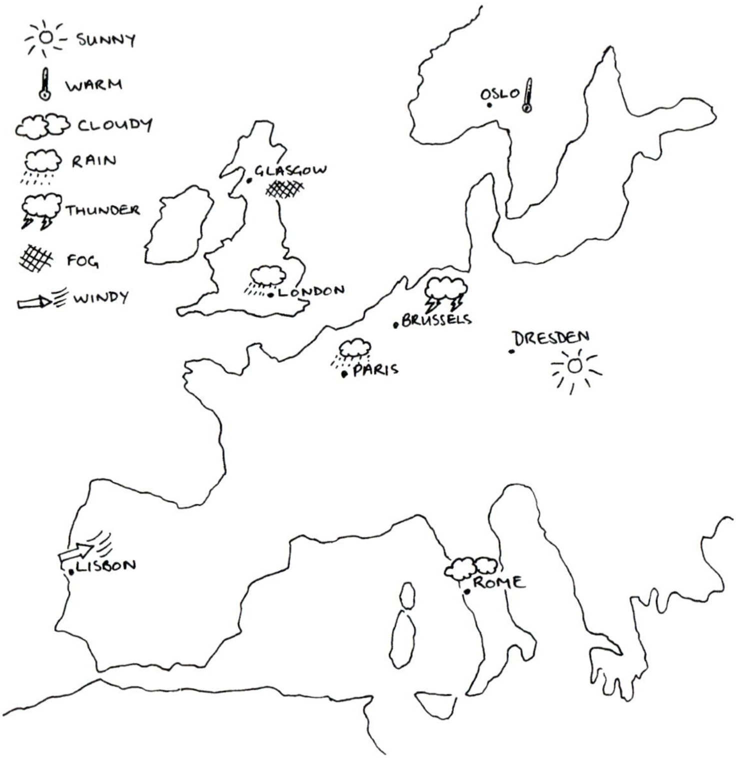

What will the weather be like? Give short answers.

1 Will it rain in London? ....

2 Will there be fog in Glasgow? ....

3 Will it be sunny in Rome? ....

4 Will the weather be cold in Oslo? ....

5 Will there be thunderstorms in Brussels? ....

6 Will it snow in Paris? ....

7 Will it be windy in Lisbon? ....

8 Will there be hail in Dresden? ....

4 A holiday

Ask the questions using question words.

how much how long when what time why how many why not how who

1 . . . . get to the hotel?
I'll get to the hotel by taxi when I arrive at the airport.

2 . . . . phone me?
What time? I'll phone you when I get to my room. But I'll be tired.

3 . . . . so tired?
Because it's quite a long flight. I won't phone my parents, though.

4 . . . . phone your parents?
Because it's too expensive, I'll send them a card.

5 . . . . when you are there?
I'll visit my friend Paolo, I expect.

6 . . . . the castle?
When? I'll go to the castle on Friday, I think.

7 . . . . for sightseeing?
How much time? I'll have lots of time I expect.

8 . . . . famous places . . . .?
How many? I don't know, but I'll visit lots of them, I'm sure.

9 . . . . on the island?
I'll be there a week.

5 The weather report

"And now this week's weather. On Monday it will be dry and sunny all day with clouds coming from the west towards evening. We'll have some very different weather on Tuesday: very windy with showers. Wednesday will be more cheerful again. Cloudy but with sunny intervals. On Thursday we'll have our first real taste of summer. Hot and sunny, with temperatures reaching 25 degrees centigrade. Friday will see a continuation of the hot weather, but towards the evening we will have the occasional thunderstorm. At the weekend it will be very changeable again, with thunderstorms and high winds all over the area. That's it from me, and back to . . ."

Will it be the right weather for them? Answer with short answers.

1 Jenny: wants to have a picnic on Tuesday.

. . . .

2 Tony: wants to go sunbathing on Thursday.

. . . .

3 Keith: wants to go on a bike tour at the weekend.

. . . .

4 Emma: wants to paint a landscape outdoors on Sunday.

. . . .

5 Roger: wants to play tennis on Wednesday.

. . . .

6 Julie: wants to go swimming in the lake on Saturday.

. . . .

6 Weather words

Which is the odd one out?

1	rain	showers	wet	fair	. . . .
2	sun	hot	snow	bright	. . . .
3	snow	humid	frost	ice	. . . .
4	thunder	fog	storm	lightning	. . . .
5	hail	hurricane	wind	breeze	. . . .
6	cloud	mist	ice	fog	. . . .

7 "als"

*How can you translate "**als**" in these sentences?*

but **than** **when** (x 2) **as** (x 3)

1 Ich war dick, **als** ich letztes Jahr hierher kam.

I was fat . . . . I came here last year.

2 Dieser Strand ist viel schöner, **als** der andere.

This beach is much more beautiful . . . . the other one.

3 **Als** Hotelmanager sind Sie sehr unhöflich!

. . . . hotel manager you are very impolite!

4 Er arbeitet **als** Reiseleiter.

He works . . . . a tour guide.

5 Es war schöner, **als** ich letztes Jahr hier war.

It was prettier . . . . I was here last year.

6 Das Hotel ist alles andere **als** sauber!

The hotel is anything . . . . clean!

7 Ich werde es dir **als** Geschenk geben.

I'll give it to . . . . a present.

8 Hotel party: The right way to say it

Which ones are right?

1 Would you like a glass wine?
Would you like a glass of wine?

2 How about going for a drink tomorrow?
Yes, I would.
That's a good idea.

3 Would you like a sandwich?
No, I wouldn't.
No, thanks.
Thank you.

4 Is that your husband over there?
Is that your man over there?

5 Those biscuits look good!
Please help yourself.
Please!

6 Would you like some dressing on your salad?
Would you like some sauce on your salad?

7 Will you dance?
Would you like a dance?

8 Would you like to go to the beach with me?
Oh, yes, I would.
Oh, yes, I'd like it.

9 Same word, different meaning

In two of these sentences you can use the same word with a different meaning. Put them in.

ring   left   glasses   right   park   too   kind   land

1 I'd like to walk through the . . . . and look at the trees.

I don't know where I can . . . . my car.

2 Don't go right at the traffic lights. Go . . . . !

Oh no! There aren't any biscuits . . . . !

3 My girlfriend is here, ...

It's . . . . hot here in the disco!

4 I'll . . . . you up on Thursday evening. Okay?

I gave her a diamond . . . ., but she left me!

5 When will your plane . . . . ?

Oh, look down there! I can see . . . . . .! It must be Australia!

6 Where are they? I can't see anything without my . . . . . . !

After the party there were so many . . . . to wash up.

7 He's so nice! He's really . . . . !

It's not that . . . . of party!

8 Take the first turning on the . . . .

I agree with you. You're . . . . !

10 Making words: -y

Put in the words in their right form.

1 Look at those snow clouds! We'll have . . . . weather tomorrow!
snow

2 I can't see anything! It's so . . . . !
fog

3 Can you feel that wind? It's so . . . . !
wind

4 Be careful on the roads today. It's very . . . .
ice

5 That plate isn't clean. It's . . . . !
dirt

6 Look at that man over there! He's really . . . . !
sex

7 I want a drink. I'm . . . . !
thirst

8 There's too much salt in this. It's really . . . .
salt

9 It's hot and . . . . here.
sun

10 It's terrible weather here! Wet and . . . . !
rain

11 Sounds

Which is the odd one out?

1	w	one	once	very	weather	. . . .
2	v	life	vegetable	live	above	. . . .
3	f	fair	wait	safe	fall	. . . .
4	w	won't	gave	will	woman	. . . .

12 Crossword: the weather

Clues

1 The sun is just so . . . . today!

2 It's not just hot and wet, it's . . . . . . !

3 I love this hot, ... weather!

4 Look at those dark clouds. I think it will . . . . soon.

5 No rain at all! It will be . . . . for the next few days.

6 It didn't rain for long. It was just a short . . . .

7 The sky is very dark and it's windy. There'll be a . . . . in a few minutes, I'm sure.

What's the word in the middle? . . . .

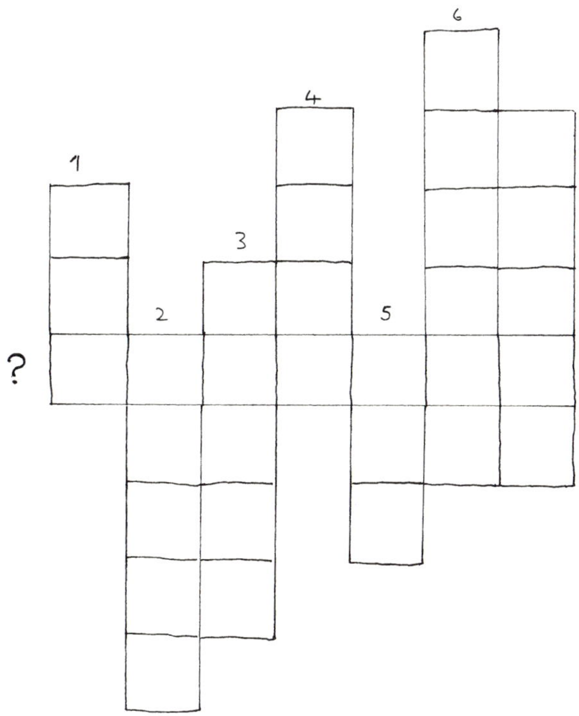

Solutions

Unit 1 Meeting People

1

1c; 2f; 3b; 4d; 5a; 6e

2

My name's Christopher. I'm not from Germany. I'm English, from London. Look, here's a photo of my family. This is my wife, Ulrike. She isn't from England. She's German. These are our children. They aren't at school yet. They are too young. And that's our dog, Toby.

3

1 Where; 2 Who; 3 Where; 4 Where; 5 Who; 6 Where

4

1 Italy; 2 Scotland; 3 England; 4 Germany; 5 France; 6 Greece; 7 Turkey; 8 Spain; 9 America; 10 Portugal

5

1:Yes, he is. 2: Yes, he has. 3: No, he hasn't. 4: Yes, she is. 5: No, she isn't. 6: No, it isn't. 7: Yes, he has. 8: No, he hasn't.

6

1: 7; 2: 21; 3: 13; 4: 30; 5: 43; 6: 12; 7: 84; 8: 96; 9: 78; 10: 59

7

1: fourteen; 2: forty; 3: fifty-six; 4: ninety-three; 5: thirty-seven; 6: seventy-three; 7: eigthy-five; 8: fifty-eight; 9: sixty-two; 10: twenty-six

8

1 there	their	3 buy	bye
2 here	hear	4 meet	meat

9

hat	**head**
cat	bed
fat	wet
sat	pet
had	said
that	set
Pat	fed
flat	

10

1 I come from Germany.
2 I live in London.
3 I work for an American firm.
4 Look at this photo.
5 I live in a big house.
6 My husband is at home all day.
7 Can I introduce you to my husband, David?

11

1 England	English	4 is	isn't
2 this	that	5 dog	cat
3 hello	goodbye	6 eight	eighty

12

1 Hello, I'm Bernd. What's your name?
2 Yes, I am.
3 Can I have your pen?
4 Here you are.

13

1: a; 2: an; 3: an; 4: a; 5: an; 6: a; 7: a

Unit 2 Home Sweet Home

1

Have you got any children?
Yes, I have.
How many children have you got?
I've got one daughter and two sons/two sons and one daughter.
Oh, that's nice.
What about you? Have you got a family?
I've got a boyfriend but we haven't got any children.
Lucky you! I'm always so busy with the kids. I just haven't got much time for myself.
I've got plenty of time! My boyfriend has got a good job. He has got a lot of free time.
My husband is always at work! He's never got any time for the family!

2

Dear David,
Thanks for your last letter. I have got some really good news!
I have got a new girlfriend! Her name's Sarah. She's wonderful! You must meet her. She has got big, blue eyes and a beautiful smile! I haven't got much time for other things at the moment, we're always together.

Have you got time next week? Perhaps we can meet. She has got an evening off next Wednesday (She has got a job as a nurse and hasn't got a lot of time in the evenings). How is Jill? Has she still got that bad cold, or is she better now? Send her my regards.
And what about you? Have you got any plans for your Summer holidays? Sarah and I have got lots of plans! I'll tell you more later.
Ring me or write me a note if you have got a moment.

3

1 Yes, he has.
2 Yes, he has.
3 No, he hasn't.
4 Yes, he has.
5 No, he hasn't.
6 Yes, he has.
7 Yes, they have.
8 No, they haven't.
9 No, he hasn't.
10 No, he hasn't.

4

2 How many rooms has your house got?
3 Has your house got a (very big) garden?
4 Have you got a swimming pool?
5 Are you very rich?
6 Do you know how much money you have got?
7 Do you know how many fans you have got?
8 Are you happy with your life?

5

1: c; 2: a; 3: b

1: Wrong; 2: Right; 3: Wrong; 4: Right; 5: Wrong; 6: Wrong

6

Gavin Richards lives in Norwich. He has got a small house ten minutes from the centre. It has got a beautiful garden with flowers and trees. "I work in it at weekends, when I have got time. It's my hobby." Gavin is separated from his wife. "She lives near here. Her house is just round the corner. We meet quite a lot, and we go out together. I phone her just about every day. It's a friendly relationship." Gavin's wife lives with their son, Ben, aged ten. Gavin sees him a lot, too. "Ben helps me with the gardening. He's very good at it! Ben, has got both of us, his father *and* his mother." Ben says: "I like them both. They are my mum and dad. But we don't live in one house. That's a pity."

7

1: near; 2: in; 3: at; 4: into; 5: in; 6: at – at; 7: down; 8: on – in front of; 9: out of; 10: in; 11: on; 12: in; 13: at; 14: in; 15: by

8

this, this, that, that, that, this, that, this, these, that, those, that, this, those, that, that

9

(Clockwise from top left)
living room, kitchen, WC/toilet, garden, bathroom, dining room

10

People: friendly, interesting, happy, ~~expensive~~, helpful, ~~empty~~
Garden: beautiful, ~~kind~~, ~~young~~, ~~handsome~~, small, boring
House: pretty, ~~young~~, expensive, ~~helpful~~, big, ~~kind~~
Sofa: comfortable, ~~sad~~, beautiful, expensive, ~~helpful~~

11

1e; 2a; 3c; 4b; 5d

12

ɑː	e
aunt	bread
fast	bed
bath	end
class	head
half	lesson
car	men
answer	

13

1: address; 2: music; 3: number; 4: paper; 5: telephone; 6: new; 7: uncle; 8: garden; 9: idea; 10: family

14

clues down	clues across
1 wife	9 father
2 mother	10 sister
3 grandmother	11 daughter
4 mum	12 aunt
5 uncle	13 brother-in-law
6 husband	14 grandad
7 son	
8 brother	

Unit 3 In Town, Out of Town

1

1 Yes, there is.
2 Yes, there are.
3 No, there isn't.
4 No, there aren't.
5 Yes, there is.
6 No, there aren't.

2

1 Is there a book shop near here?
2 Is there a florist's near here/in town?
3 Are there any art galleries here/near here/in town?
4 Is there a baker's near here?
5 Are there any restaurants near here?
6 Is there an underground station here/near hear/round here?

3

Dear Jenny,
We're in our new house now; it's super! We haven't got any curtains yet, but we've got some really wonderful furniture: a sofa, two armchairs, a dining table and some chairs. The street's quite quiet. There isn't any traffic at night, but there are some noisy neighbours next door! They're quite friendly, but they often have friends round, and they play some very loud music at times. There is a nice Pakistani family across the street, though. They've got some sweet children! I don't think they've got any friends around here. They're happy to meet some new people, like us.
What about you? Have you got any news?

4

stays, watches, likes, listens, wants, does, sits, hurries, helps, relaxes, has, tries, comes, kisses, says

5

3 Adrian doesn't play tennis.
4 Thomas doesn't listen to classical music.
5 Adrian doesn't like dancing.
6 Thomas doesn't play chess.
7 Adrian doesn't go out a lot.

8 Thomas doesn't stay at home a lot.
9 Adrian doesn't read magazines.
10 Thomas doesn't read books.
11 Adrian doesn't watch TV.
12 Thomas doesn't collect stamps.

6

1 Do you do a lot of sports?
2 What sports do you do?
3 Do you go out with friends?
4 Do you ever go to the theatre?
5 Do you ever watch films at the cinema?
6 Do you ever go to restaurants?
7 Do you ever go for walks?
8 Do you ever drive to work?
9 Do you ever watch TV?

7

1: block of flats; 2: cottage; 3: semidetached house; 4: stately home; 5: terraced house; 6 detached house; 7: bungalow; 8: bed-sitter

8

Going out	**Staying in**
restaurant	sofa
park	chess
jogging	radio
cinema	TV
walk	living room
disco	relax
tennis club	video
pub	lazy

9

in, into, to, in, at, next to, in, in front of, through, down

10

1 He goes into town every day.
2 She lives on the second floor.
3 You can buy it at the supermarket.
4 They are at the cinema.
5 Welcome to London!
6 She is on the bus to Norwich.

11

go to the shops, out with friends, for a walk, by bus
do the shopping, sports, the washing up, the housework
watch a video, TV, a film
listen to CDs, the radio, music

12

1: helps; 2: stays; 3: asks; 4: makes; 5: plays

13

Dear Granny,
It's nice here on holiday. It's a lovely house. There are lots of nice things here and a cinema next door and a park down the road. Mum and Dad are all right. They're in the garden now with friends. Today I want to buy a comic. How are you?

14

shops, bank, post office, supermarket, cinema, disco, restaurant, bus stop, park, street

Unit 4 From Day to Day

1

1: by bus; 2: by train; 3: on foot; 4: by car; 5: by underground/tube

2

1: Right; 2: Wrong; 3: Right; 4: Wrong; 5: Wrong; 6: Wrong; 7: Right

3

1 My wife works in an office.
2 She's a secretary.
3 She's got a nice boss, and her colleagues are all right, too.
4 I do the shopping because she gets home quite late.
5 At the weekend she's got time for the family.
6 During the week she's always tired in the evening.
7 On Saturdays we go out together.
8 That's the best day of the week, I think.
9 Our two little boys are often sad because she's away all day.
10 I do all the jobs in the house because I'm out of work.

4

1 What do you do?/What's your job?
2 Is it a hard job?
3 When/What time do you get up?
4 When/What time do you make breakfast (for the family)?
5 When/What time do you start your housework?
6 Do you have a break?
7 When/What time is your coffee break?
8 When/What time do you cook lunch?
9 When/What time does your husband get home?
10 When/What time does your son get back from school?
11 What do you do in the evenings?
12 When/What time do you go to bed?

5

a)

1 

2 

3 

4 

b)

5 half past seven
6 five to four (pm)
7 (a) quarter to twelve
8 twenty-five past nine

6

1: to, at; 2: from; 3: between; 4: from . . . to; 5: in; 6: until; 7: at

7

1: photocopier; 2: typewriter; 3: computer; 4: desk; 5: printer; 6: chair; 7: fax; 8: calculator; 9: telephone

8

1: for; 2: at; 3: near; 4: at; 5: with

9

1: typewriter; 2: bike; 3: week; 4: secretary; 5: interesting

10

5

11

ð	θ
that	through
rather	thirteen
those	bath
father	thirty
these	thanks
there	throw

12

1: manager; 2: nurse; 3: doctor; 4: teacher; 5: policeman; 6: waiter; 7: engineer; 8: secretary; 9: butcher

Unit 5 Time for Fun

1

mine, hers, my; their, our, theirs; your, ours; her, his, his

2

1: can't stand; 2: like; 3: love; 4: don't like

3

1b; 2d; 3c; 4a

4

1 How old are you?
2 Are you an active person?
3 Do you like sports?
4 What sports do you do?
5 Have you got any other interests?
6 Can you play an instrument?
7 Do you like classical music?
8 What sort of music do you like?
9 Where do you live?
10 What sort of woman do you like?
11 Do you like going to the cinema?

5

1 Where do you go every evening?
To the tennis club.
2 Who do you play with?
I always play with my boyfriend.
3 When/How often does your husband watch TV?
Every day. It's terrible!
4 How much does the Cezanne exhibition cost?
About £5, I think.
5 How do they go on holiday?
They go by train. They haven't got a car.
6 Why does she like disco music so much? I think it's awful!
Because she loves dancing.

7 How often do you take your dog for a walk?
Twice a day.
8 What does he like about Susan?
Well, she's an active person, like he is. And she's very intelligent.
9 What time/When does the film start?
At eight o'clock.

6

2: 3rd; 3: 42nd; 4: 30th; 5: 4th; 6: 99th; 7: 11th; 8: 13th; 9: 31st; 10: 60th

7

1: fifth; 2: thirty-third; 3: twelfth; 4: fortieth; 5: fourteenth; 6: fifty-first; 7: twenty-second; 8: eighth; 9: fifteenth; 10: hundredth

8

1: Shrove Tuesday, or "Pancake Day"; 2: Christmas Day; 3: Christmas Day; 4: Guy Fawkes Night

9

+	–
interesting	boring
good	awful
friendly	bad
beautiful	terrible
excellent	unfriendly
fantastic	dangerous
wonderful	silly
exciting	stupid

10

1: chief; 2: January; 3: catch; 4: orange

11

1: footballer; 2: player; 3: driver; 4: joggers; 5: runners; 6: computer; 7: singer; 8: painter

12

INDOORS	OUTDOORS
playing tennis	playing tennis
watching TV	jogging
playing chess	climbing
doing the washing up	skiing
playing squash	basketball
collecting stamps	reading books
basketball	sunbathing
listening to the radio	
playing computer games	
reading books	
bodybuilding	

13

1: tell; 2: interesting; 3: mean; 4: think; 5: interested; 6: do; 7: tells; 8: making; 9: make; 10: do

14

A	N	D	O	X	I	N	M	O	F	G
O	J	O	G	G	I	N	G	R	O	T
L	I	T	F	A	H	C	S	T	F	O
T	K	N	O	S	S	T	I	R	F	Y
E	O	F	F	I	T	R	U	E	B	Y
N	F	C	H	E	S	S	U	A	A	B
N	C	K	O	L	S	Y	O	D	B	A
I	I	S	L	O	P	O	R	I	F	O
S	T	M	U	S	I	C	T	N	B	Y
T	I	F	F	I	R	G	A	G	C	U
F	O	O	T	B	A	L	L	N	F	O

Unit 6 Going Out

1

To be crossed out:
someone; nowhere; anybody; someone; anything; anyone's; something; noone; anything; somebody; anywhere; anywhere; nowhere; somewhere; anywhere

2

I'd like, I like, I like, I like, I'd like, I like, I like, I'd like, I'd like, I like.

3

Would you like to go out this evening?
Oh, yes. I would. That's a great idea.
Would you like to go to the cinema?
Not really. I don't really like going to the cinema.
What would you like to do?
What about a meal?
Good idea! Would you like to try the new Indian restaurant?
Oh, yes, I'd like that. I love curry!
Let's meet there at eight.
Fine. See you later!

4

Would you like to go out with me this evening?
Would you like to go to the Italian restaurant?
Do you like dancing?
Would you like to go to the disco?
Do you like the one in King Street?
Would you like a lift there?

5

1 Yes, please.
2 No, thanks.
3 Yes, I love it.
4 Actually, I don't really like Spanish food.
5 Would you like a dance?

6

1: Wrong; 2: Right; 3: Wrong; 4: Wrong; 5: Right; 6: Right; 7: Wrong; 8: Wrong

7

To be underlined:
1: pint of bitter; 2: box of matches; 3: mineral water; 4: ashtray; 5: barman

8

1: for; 2: at; 3: at; 4: to; 5: at; 6: in; 7: back; 8: in; 9: out; 10: on

9

æ	ɑː
back	glass
happy	half
beermat	bar
hat	party
flat	ask

10

impossible, unable, unfriendly, unusual, impolite, uninteresting, inefficient, inexpensive, uncomfortable, impersonal, unrealistic

11

1: Look; 2: watch; 3: see; 4: Look; see; 5: looks; 6: look; 7: See; 8: watches; 9: looking; 10: see

12

1: orange juice; 2: water; 3: beer; 4: bitter lemon; 5: lemonade; 6: whisky

Unit 7 Daily Bread

1

12, 8, 5, 10, 7, 2, 3, 9, 6, 11, 4, 1

2

1: £6.75; 2: £10.62; 3: £21.25; 4: £1.82

3

1: £3.57; 2: £5.77; 3: £5.71

4

1: How many; 2: How much; 3: How much; 4: How many;
5: How much; 6: How many; 7: How much; 8: How many

5

1 are cheaper than
2 is fresher than
3 is more expensive than
4 is saltier than
5 is hotter than
6 more interesting than
7 better than
8 nicer than
9 are worse
10 are bigger than

6

Yes. I'd like a jar of jam, please.
I'd like strawberry jam, please.
Yes. I'd like a kilo of potatoes, please.
Thank you. How much is that altogether?

7

1: Wrong; 2: Wrong; 3: Right; 4: Right; 5: Wrong; 6: Wrong

8

1 Hello.
2 I'd like a kilo of tomatoes, please.
3 I'd like a grapefruit, too, please.
4 How much does a lettuce cost?

5 How much is that altogether?
6 Put the money in the shopkeeper's hand.
7 Here you are.

9

a jar of jam
a packet of crisps, biscuits, cornflakes
a box of matches
a bottle of cola, milk
a tin of cola, biscuits, milk, baked beans
a can of cola, baked beans
a tube of toothpaste
a roll of toilet paper
a bag of crisps
a bar of chocolate, soap
a loaf of bread

10

newsagent's	**baker's**	**chemist's/drugstore**	**butcher's**
magazines	bread	cosmetics	meat
newspapers	cake	toiletries	sausages
cigarettes	rolls	medicine	

11

2: vegetables; 3: meat; 4: fruit

12

eə	ɪə	ɜː
where	here	sir
pair	near	burn
wear	clear	turn
pear	hear	fair

13

2: breakable; 3: edible; 4: enjoyable; 5: disposable; 6: visible

14

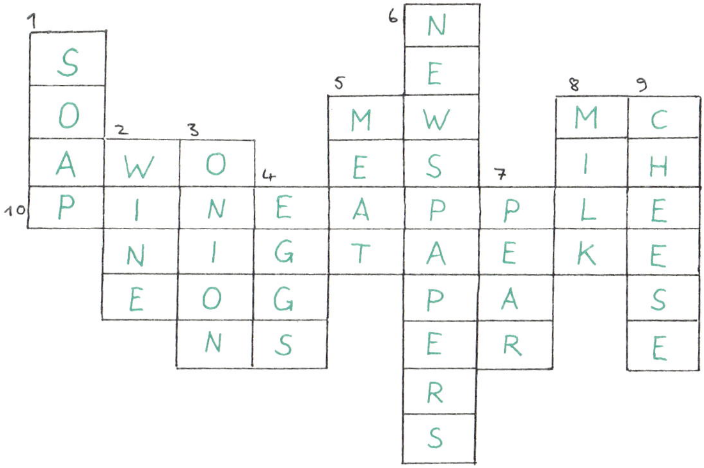

Unit 8 Stores and Floors

1

1: much; 2: many; 3: much; 4: many; 5: much; 6: much

2

1c; 2a; 3d; 4e; 5f; 6b

3

latest; best; worst; most comfortable; lightest; least expensive; largest; most fashionable; biggest.

4

one; ones; one; one; ones; ones; ones; one; one; one; ones

5

on; next to; between, behind; on; through; at the bottom; on; downstairs

6

1 in the sports department on the second floor
2 on the fifth floor
3 in the menswear department on the first floor
4 in the cosmetics department on the ground floor
5 in the furniture department on the fourth floor
6 in the ladies' wear department on the third floor
7 the electrical goods department on the third floor
8 the toys department on the fourth floor

7

1: hat; 2: shirt; 3: tie; 4: jacket; 5: trousers; 6: blouse; 7: shoes; 8: skirt; 9: socks

8

2: beautiful; 3: peaceful; 4: careless; 5: endless; 6: colourful; 7: helpful; 8: useful; 9: useless; 10: speechless; 11: playful; 12: harmless

9

colourless; untidy; ugly; large; narrow; short; loose; soft; dark; uncomfortable

10

ɪ	iː
women	key
sit	canteen
system	eat
lift	cheap
little	scene
fifty	field

11

1: How; 2: as; 3: What; 4: like; 5: like; 6: What

12

P	S	H	I	R	T	C	K
L	F	U	S	H	O	E	S
T	R	O	U	S	E	R	S
D	O	S	O	C	K	S	T
R	S	K	I	R	T	U	I
E	F	F	Y	O	B	A	E
S	J	A	C	K	E	T	A
S	S	T	R	D	S	F	O

Unit 9 **Eating Out**

1

4; 9; 3; 10; 1; 7; 8; 5; 2; 6

2

Bob	**Jim**
shrimp cocktail	shrimp cocktail
fillet steak	grilled plaice
chips	boiled potatoes
green salad	peas
pint of lager	glass of white wine

3

To be crossed out:
get; in; with; want; is it; will; recipe

4

1: I'll; 2: I'd; 3: I'll; 4: I'll; 5: I'd; 6: I'll

5

at; at; in; on; to; with; on; under; up; off

6

1 Can I have the menu, please?
2 Can I have some bread, please?
3 I'll have the apple pie, please.
4 Waiter!
5 No, thanks.
6 A glass of wine for my wife, please.
7 I'd like a dessert, please.
8 Can I have the bill, please?

7

1: True; 2: False; 3: False; 4: False; 5: True; 6: False; 7: True; 8: False

8

2: undercooked; 3: overpriced; 4: overcharged; 5: overworked; 6: underpaid; 7: overdone

9

1:bill; 2: wineglass; 3: pepper; 4: salt; 5: menu; 6: winelist; 7: fork; 8: plate; 9: dessert spoon; 10: sideplate; 11: knife; 12: soup spoon; 13: napkin

10

1: delicious; 2: awful; 3: burnt; 4: tough; 5: tender; 6: salty; 7: hot (spicy); 8: bland; 9: sweet; 10: tasty

11

1: table; 2: walk

12

dessert; bill; menu; knife; plate; fork; steak; waiter

Unit 10 Away from Home

1

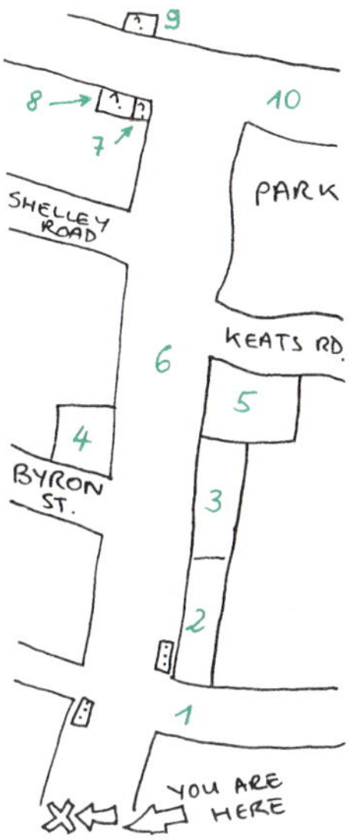

1: Milton Road
2: Bank
3: Café
4: Supermarket
5: Record Shop
6: High Street
7: Fish and Chip Shop
8: Post Office
9: Chemist's
10: Park Road

2

1e; 2d; 3b; 4f; 5a; 6c

3

1 Go straight on
2 Go down
3 Turn left into
4 Take the second turning
5 Cross the road

4

1 on the corner
2 next to the bank
3 opposite the bank
4 between the florist's and the bank
5 near the bank

5

Good morning. Marina hotel. Can I help you?
Good morning. I'd like to book a room, please.
When is it for?
It's for next Friday and Saturday – the 3rd and 4th.
Would you like a single room or a double room?
A double room, please.
With a bath or a shower?
With a shower. How much is the room?
It's £80 a night.
Does that include breakfast?
Yes, it does. Could I have your name, please?
It's Martin, Mr and Mrs Martin.
Thank you, Mrs Martin.

6

1: Show; 2: Take; 3: Don't drop; 4: Don't be; 5: Be; 6: Get; 7: Stop; 8: Don't smoke

7

for; on; in; at; on; with; of; to

8

1: False; 2: False; 3: True; 4: True; 5: False; 6: True; 7: True; 8: False

9

1 Excuse me, can you tell me where the park is?
2 Excuse me, is there a bank near here?
3 Can you tell me the way to the post office?
4 The butcher's is next to the supermarket.
5 The bus stop is in front of the pub.
6 You're welcome.

10

1: nearest; 2: next; 3: next; 4: next; 5: nearest; 6: nearest; 7: next

11

iː	aɪ
street	guide
feet	size
field	buy
meet	bike
scene	try
key	arrive

12

1: waitress; 2: manageress; 3: sportswoman; 4: Frenchwoman; 5: saleswoman; 6: stewardess; 7: actress; 8: policewoman

13

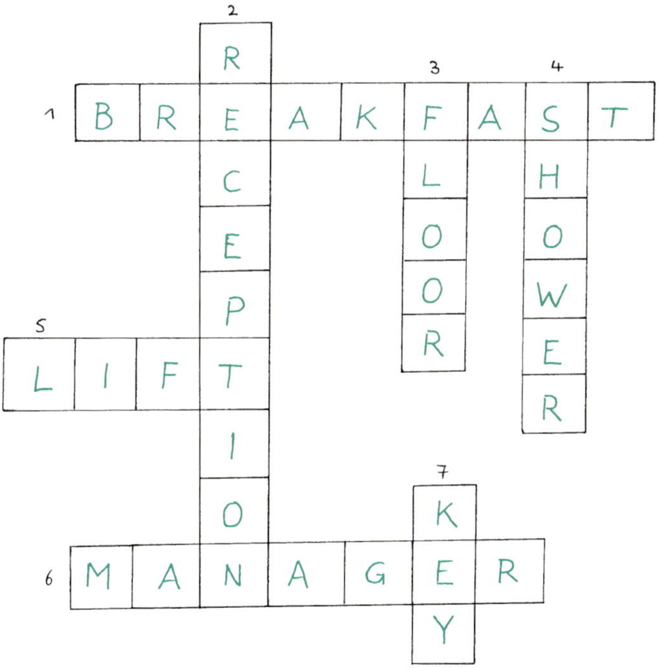

Unit 11 Up and Away

1

"It was so wonderful! We were in a really modern hotel with a swimming pool, but there weren't any people in it because the beach was so beautiful. I wasn't in the water very much because I can't swim very well, but the children were in and out of the sea all day!
The food was delicious, and those waiters! Well, they were charming and very good-looking! Tom wasn't very well on the last day. In fact, we were all a little bit ill for a while. It was too hot. Anyway, what was your holiday in Clacton like?"

2

1 Yes, it was.
2 Yes, they were.
3 Yes, it was.
4 No, they weren't.
5 Yes, they were.
6 No, it wasn't.
7 No, they weren't.
8 Yes, we were.
9 Yes, she was.
10 No, he wasn't.

3

1 What was the weather like?
2 How was the hotel?
3 Why was it so loud?
4 Where was the hotel?
5 How much was your hired car?
6 How many people were on the beach?
7 When were you at the famous castle?
8 Who was there to meet you at the airport when you got back?

4

arrived; checked; looked; were; was; walked; watched; talked; showed; played

5

at; on; at; to; in; on; at; in; under; along; at; over; by

6

1: True; 2: True; 3: False; 4: True; 5: True; 6: False; 7: True

7

1 I need a pair of sunglasses.
2 I want to buy a pair of swimming trunks.
3 We must get a sunshade.
4 Careful! You've got sunburn!
5 It's cool here in the shade.

8

9

1: sunglasses; 2: suntan lotion; 3: suntan; 4: sunshade; 5: sunshine; 6: sunstroke; 7: sunbathe; 8: sunburn

10

d	t	ɪd
lived	worked	started
stayed	looked	wanted
arrived	finished	hated
showed	watched	waited

11

1 We were in Crete a week ago.
2 He sat in front of the TV in the evenings.
3 We went to the beach before breakfast.
4 A year ago we were in Italy.
5 We walked along the beach before sunset.

12

1: beach; 2: deckchair; 3: sunglasses; 4: wave; 5: sunshade; 6: sunburn

Unit 12 The Big City

1

buy bought	take took	get got
eat ate	meet met	have had
do did	see saw	be was/were
drink drank	speak spoke	say said
go went	travel travelled	

2

was; went; took; looked; did; got; had; ate; said; was; met; spoke; told; loved; went; saw; found; tried; travelled

3

1 I didn't see the Tower of London.
2 We didn't have a late lunch.
3 I didn't like Trafalgar Square.
4 I didn't take a lot of photos.
5 I didn't buy any souvenirs.
6 We didn't find the Science Museum very interesting.
7 We didn't go to St. Paul's Cathedral.
8 The weather wasn't very good.

4

1 Yes, we/I did.
2 No, we/I didn't.
3 No, he didn't.
4 Yes, we/I did.
5 No, it wasn't.
6 No, we/I didn't.
7 No, it didn't.
8 Yes, we/I did.

5

1 Did you like London?
2 Did you go shopping?
3 Did you travel by tube?
4 Did you visit the British Museum?
5 Did you see any speakers at Speaker's Corner?
6 Did you take any photos?
7 Did you buy any souvenirs?
8 Did you have a good day out?

6

Sentence 4 is wrong.

7

To be crossed out:
1: between; 2: straight on; 3: on; 4: next; 5: in; 6: with; 7: by; 8: before; 9: of; 10: opposite

8

1: tube; 2: street map; 3: river; 4: film; 5: postcard; 6: bus; 7: art gallery; 8: cinema

9

1: weekend; 2: sightsee; 3: underground; 4: timetable; 5: alleyway; 6: supermarket; 7: bathroom; 8: footstep; 9: churchyard; 10: riverside

10

To be crossed out:
1: does; 2: does; 3: make; 4: did; 5: made; 6: make; 7: makes; 8: does

11

American; Russian; Brazilian; Australian; Italian; Austrian; Sicilian; Hungarian; Chilean; European; Canadian; Moroccan; Belgian; Argentinian

12

To be underlined:
shout; four; crowd; port

13

1: tour; 2: London; 3: guide; 4: underground; 5: information; 6: bus; 7: ticket
The word is: tourist

Unit 13 Last Night ...

1

said; wanted; did ... speak; saw; had; didn't look; looked; met; bought; didn't sound; broke; liked; wasn't; went; tried; did ... get; wanted; didn't

2

1 What was the party like?
2 Who did you go with?
3 Where did you meet her?
4 When/What time did you get to the party?
5 Why did you arrive late?
6 What did Lisa wear?
7 How many people came to the party?
8 How long did it go on for?
9 How did you get home?

3

1g; 2d; 3a; 4f; 5b; 6c; 7e

4

To be crossed out:
there; as; for; on; into; near of; over here; to; to; forward; along; for; by; with us; outside; below; from; on; at

5

Last Friday I went to a party at Jon and Tina's friend's house. It started at 7.30 am and was really boring at the beginning. Then guests started to arrive. There were a lot of people because they all brought their parents. They all wore fancy dress in red and black. There was a lot to eat and drink because everybody brought a barrel of beer and some sandwiches.

6

disc jockey; disco music; party dress; admission fee; phone call; wine bar; ice cream; credit card; traveller's cheque; swimming pool

7

To be crossed out:
1: here, hear; 2: there, their; 3: too, two; 4: new, knew; 5: red, read; 6: hour, our; 7: sea, see; 8: sun, son; 9: weak, week; 10: weight, wait

8

1 listen
2 listened
3 hear
4 hear
5 hear
6 Listen
7 listens
8 heard
9 listen, hear

9

1 Fine, thanks. And you?
2 That's a very attractive woman over there.
3 I'd like you to meet my husband.
4 Let me buy you a drink.
5 That man is my husband's colleague.
6 Look at that tie he's wearing!
7 There are lots of people here.

8 Let's meet next week.
9 Yes, see you then.
10 You, too!

10

1 unhappy	5 unimportant	8 illogical
2 impossible	6 impolite	9 unclear
3 dislike	7 informal	10 irregular
4 disagree		

11

ago; edge; guest; jump

12

1 disc jockey	3 lights
2 music	4 dance

Unit 14 Looking Forward

1

1d; 2h; 3a; 4f; 5b; 6k; 7i; 8j; 9c; 10g; 11e

2

2 You will win a lot of money on the lottery.
3 You will live to be very old.
4 Your husband will get a very good job.
5 You won't be ill this winter.
6 Your daughter will marry a famous actor.
7 Your husband won't watch football on TV again.
8 You will move to a luxury villa.

3

1 Yes, it will.	4 No, it won't.	7 Yes, it will.
2 Yes, there will.	5 Yes, there will.	8 No, there won't.
3 No, it won't.	6 No, it won't.	